FORGIVING A FAE WARRIOR

MEGAN VAN DYKE

Author's Note

Forgiving a Fae Warrior is book 2.5 in the Courts of Faery series and is intended as a companion novel to book 2. This novella is told from Galen's point of view, starting with the events of chapter 36 from *Bound to the Fae King*, and continuing past the end of that novel.

It is strongly encouraged that you read both book 1, *A Bargain with the Fae King*, and book 2, *Bound to the Fae King*, before beginning this story as it contains significant spoilers for both books. Furthermore, portions of this story will not make sense without the background and events presented in those books that leads up to this novella.

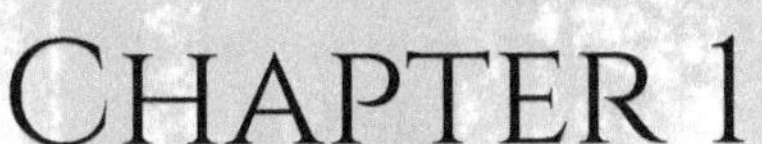

CHAPTER 1

G ALEN SAT ON A bench with his head in his hands as the long night drew toward morning. Dawn wouldn't be too far off, but the sounds of the party to celebrate the end of the annual games still carried through the night. Some would drink and dance well into the next day. By rights, he should have been one of them—he had much to be thankful for. He'd beaten dozens of others to make it to the final trial, and though he hadn't won, he could have.

The answer to the final question had struck him like a bolt of lightning. *Trust.* He was so certain of it that the word rose to the tip of his tongue and would have spilled out into the tent where the final game was held if one of the other contestants hadn't chosen that moment to shout their guess. During the full silence that hung in the air before their answer was deemed incorrect, Galen had spied Wren, the human woman who had made it to the finals against all odds.

The utter devastation written on her face twisted something sharp in his middle. Winning was her one way home, the only way to break the bond that Sigurd, King of Air, had imposed upon her. If she lost, that chance would be gone. She'd be forced to remain in Faery until the bond faded, which could take years. The family she left behind didn't have that kind of time, and Galen knew all too well the pain of being separated from loved ones. It was why he entered the competition after all.

Every day he thought of Sylvie, the woman he loved and had left behind when he fled the Court of the Forest after betraying its king, all at the orders of Sigurd, King of Air.

Years ago, Galen's father had been insistent that his son follow in his footsteps as a loyalist to the Court of Air, serving their king by vow while living amongst the Forest Court. As a child born of two courts, Forest and Air, he could belong to either or both. But Galen wasn't quite like his father. He never had been. He took the vow to Sigurd to please his parents, never thinking that it would one day be called in, that he would be forced to betray the king and court he had chosen to follow—his home, his true family, and that of the woman he loved.

No one could reverse time, but if he were able, he'd go back and convince his younger self to save all his oaths for Sylvie.

The winner of the competition could drink from the ancient cauldron and have a wish granted. It could deem his oath fulfilled and allow him to return to the Court of the Forest. They may not want him there, not after what he'd done, but he'd do everything in his power to see Sylvie again, even just one more time.

She was fierce, confident, a bright spot of light in any room she entered. The human woman Wren was much the same with her determination and inner strength that he couldn't help but admire her, and she'd been loyal to him throughout the games.

Wren had once claimed that she could convince Sigurd to free him of his vow. Though Galen loathed and doubted the man, those feelings did not extend to Wren, even if she somehow found it in her heart to care for the king who'd made him a traitor in the eyes of the Forest and the woman he loved.

Sigurd had betrayed Wren, too, in a way, binding her to him through ill magic and preventing Wren from returning to the human world and her family there. But still, she found it in her to care for him, to trust him. And so, when Galen puzzled out the riddle in the final game, he did exactly what the answer instructed—he trusted. Wren had only one way home, but he might have another if she could convince the king to free him as she believed.

By some stroke of luck, Wren had noticed him as he stared at her during that last trial as his heart threatened to hammer out of his chest. She understood the word he mouthed to her. Every second that passed, someone else might have figured out the answer and spoken it aloud to claim victory.

But they didn't.

Wren won and held true. She asked the king to fulfill the wishes of the other finalists if he could, and by some miracle, Sigurd agreed. That included removing the balance of the oath Galen had long ago sworn to Sigurd. He was free now, but the shackles on his soul felt heavy as ever, pressing on his shoulders and squeezing his chest like a band of iron.

The lingering force of his vow to Sigurd gave had given him a goal: be released of it. But he hadn't stopped to think of what came next. With the vow gone, there were no excuses to keep him from facing down the consequences of his actions, and that was an even more brutal struggle to overcome. Nothing stopped him from returning to the Court of the Forest right that moment. Nothing...but himself.

If he returned now, would they bother to hear him out before slaying him on the spot as a traitor? He couldn't be sure.

In all his musings, only one of the potential ideas that had developed in his mind glimmered with the possibility of success. It was risky in so many ways and would be difficult to achieve, but it was something. And so, he clung to that little thread of hope and followed it through, adjusting his steps as he went along.

Galen sighed and shifted on the bench. That plan was the reason he'd chosen this particular spot. Not far away loomed the tent of the King of Air, his elite guards posted around the outside to ensure his safety and privacy on this night. Wren was in there with him. He knew without being told, though his suspicions were confirmed when he inquired with the guards.

He might not understand her love for the king who had bound her to this court, but the king's willingness to break tradition and grant the wishes of the finalists—to the extent he could—showed exactly how much he cared for her.

By any luck, he'd be able to see Wren again before Sigurd stole her away to his castle or let her return to her world. Though she might love the king, Galen knew it wouldn't stop her from returning to care for her family. It was just one more thing he admired about her.

Perhaps without Sigurd in the way, they could have been friends. She'd called him such, and though he wanted the same, the winged specter of the king would always be an obstacle between them.

Not to mention that she would probably loathe him after this night.

As if his thoughts summoned her, Wren exited the king's tent alone. Even from a distance, he could make out her tousled hair and rumbled clothing. His cheeks heated, and he forced himself to look away—back down at his boots.

Galen pulled in one deep breath after another, trying to steady the nerves threatening to tear him apart. His fingers dug into his hairline almost painfully as he grappled for control of his emotions.

Have courage.

The crunch of footsteps, barely audible over the lingering noise of the party coming from some distance behind him, alerted Galen of the guards' approach with Wren. They would have told her his request to meet with her, and kind woman that she was, she came to see him.

But even if not for that sound, he would have felt her approach. She bore Sigurd's mark now, so much stronger and more acute a thing than the bond he'd placed on her before, which the cauldron had removed as part of her victory. Sigurd's scent clung to her, drifting along the faint night breeze and turning his stomach.

She was more than just a human favored by the king now. She was his chosen, his bonded mate, possibly even his future queen. After all, the king, for all his faults, wasn't known to take lovers, particularly not human ones. Wren was different. Special. Not only that, as a human, she would strengthen his magic and that of the entire court. She was a wise choice, and Sigurd did care for the well-being of the Court of Air.

"Thank you," Wren said to a guard. "I'll be fine with my friend."

Her friend. The title only made everything worse.

Galen raised his head as the guards moved away. They wouldn't go far. Not only were humans valuable and treasured, Wren was as precious as their king now that she shared his mark. Even so, they'd give them the illusion of privacy since she asked for it.

Wren looked from the retreating guards to Galen. "I thought you'd have left by now."

"I wanted to see you again first," he replied.

A soft smile rose to her lips. Her posture loosened in what could only be relief.

She wanted to see me. Another thing so simple and natural but more painful than she could ever know.

Wren was here, but soon she would be gone, and he would lose his chance. He couldn't let that happen. Galen rose to his feet and offered her his arm. "Walk with me?"

"Please," she replied, sliding her arm through his. Like a companion, a friend. Galen swallowed against the tightness in his throat.

The guards followed at a distance. Galen attuned himself to their presence, the sound of their footsteps, leaning into his many years of training as a member of the elite guard of the Forest.

"He marked you," Galen said as they walked, the accusation coming out much harsher than he intended.

Wren's arm through his stiffened ever so slightly. "It was mutual." She gave a half-shrug as if it was nothing important, but the words and the act spoke volumes.

The king's desire for her was obvious. And while his scent often clung to her, Wren had seemed uncertain, more torn by whatever connection they had and still steadfast on returning home. Had that changed?

"So you won't be leaving after all?" Galen asked, his curiosity piqued. "You win the tournament for your freedom and then decide to stay?" The last bit came out edged in bitterness. She'd done as she promised, yes, but trying so hard to win just to give it up? The thought had his jaw clenching tight.

"No," Wren snapped, raising her chin and standing a little taller. "I still plan to return home. In the morning, in fact."

Galen nearly missed a step as her reaction sank home. So soon, despite the mark she shared with the king. If he'd waited, he'd have been too late, just as he feared. Time was rarely his ally, and the lack of it only strengthened his resolve.

"My family needs me. That hasn't changed," Wren continued. "I plan to go home and care for them, see that they're well."

Good. He was glad of it. She hadn't changed her mind or waivered in her determination despite whatever passed between her and the king. No matter what happened in the future or what she might think of him after this night, he was glad that she stayed true to herself.

"And then?" he asked. It was dangerous to give himself an out, a possible second chance if things did not go according to his plan. Still, he couldn't help but wonder.

"I want to come back." She gave another half-shrug. "Maybe go back and forth for a while."

"I see."

But his thoughts had drifted inward. Every possible negative outcome taunted him. There was one thing she had to know, though. Something that must be said before anything else.

"Thank you, Wren, for asking for our wishes."

"It's nothing," she replied.

"It's so much more than that. You had such confidence that the king would listen to your request, but I still doubted it. I thought, at best, it might be a deception, something to make it seem like my oath was revoked but holding me here just the same. But it's not. I'm truly free." The last part trails off into a breathy whisper. Free of the vow? Yes. Truly free? So far from it.

A burst of laughter from further down the path interrupted the silence hanging between them. He'd led them toward the party, the crowds, hoping the music and conversation would cloak some of their words, that the dancing flames and their shadows might give him a few precious extra moments.

"I'm happy for you," Wren said with a smile. "You can return to Sylvie."

Without thought, Galen reached up to rub the little golden leaf dangling from his ear. Though she would be far, far away, whatever enchantment clung to the gift still gave a tiny pull in her direction. The momentary joy sparked by her name slipped away as quickly as it came, the metal suddenly cold under his touch. Even if he managed to see her again, she may never forgive him. He might never see her smile, hear her laughter, or enjoy the blessing of her company.

"If she'll have me," he mumbled. "If any of them will after what I've done."

He slipped his arm from Wren's as fear tried to steal the last of his resolve. He turned away, breathing deeply and willing his racing heart to calm.

"Forgiveness can take time. It may not be immediate, but once they hear your story, it may come sooner than you expect."

Galen huffed air through his nose but met Wren's determined stare.

"My Uncle Mark, Hawke's mate, left my family. Just up and disappeared one day. We didn't know why or where he'd gone or even if he was alive," she said.

Something moved in the shadows behind Wren, almost like a form slipping silently between two seemingly empty tents. The fine hairs on the back of Galen's neck rose. He scanned for the guards, finding them absent. Perhaps they hid just out of sight?

"It's true," Wren continued. "I was so angry with him for years for leaving like that. But I found him here. I heard his story. It doesn't make what he did right, but I understand his side of it, why he did what he did. If a few conversations can help overcome years of hurt and pain, then I'm sure they can do the same for you."

"Perhaps," he mused, staring off toward the nearest group of partiers and finding nothing amiss. "But they'll have to listen to me first."

Wren's sudden intake of breath grabbed his attention. "Galen." She tugged at his sleeve. "Did you see that?"

"See what?" The calm words belied the tingling feeling racing across his skin and the rapid thrum of the blood through his veins. The shadows were still, but he couldn't shake the feeling he had a moment ago or dismiss the lack of guards. Something was amiss, especially if Wren noticed it too.

"I thought I saw someone."

As did he. The guards wouldn't be so secretive, and anyone else—

"I should go back. It's late." Wren turned back toward Sigurd's tent.

The simple move snapped Galen from his worries, and he stopped her with a hand on her arm. "Wait."

She turned to him and blinked innocently.

Shit. He needed a reason to stop her, and so, he spoke the worry he couldn't shake, "You truly think betrayal can be forgiven?" His pulse hammered wildly in his chest. A little voice screamed in the back of his mind to act. The surge of emotion let out a soft glow from his eyes which he couldn't hold back.

"Yes, I truly do."

He nodded and swallowed hard. "Good." Maybe she would forgive him too someday. Galen took her hand in his and squeezed. "Because I am so sorry about this, Wren."

CHAPTER 2

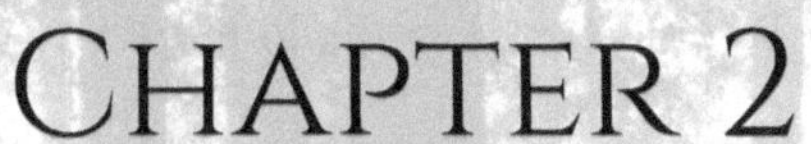

G ALEN FLUNG HIS MAGIC out to encompass Wren. Such a long shift, to the edge of the Court of the Forest, was taxing. It would have been easier if he had rested and prepared, but the idea for how to possibly earn forgiveness from the Court of the Forest, or at least the chance to explain himself, hadn't fully taken shape until that evening as he'd wandered the celebration aimlessly, lost in thought. The moment his footsteps had taken him to Sigurd's tent—to Wren—he knew with sick certainty what would give the Court of Forest pause and show their king where his loyalties lay.

He'd repent and earn forgiveness in the same way he'd become a traitor—one human woman to atone for another.

Finally, the pull on his magic faded, and Galen's feet settled on solid ground. Wren stumbled and slipped, but he held her firm, refusing to let her fall.

"How dare—" She began.

"You'll be safe," Galen assured her. "The Court of the Forest will get you home." No harm would ever come to her at the hands of those in the Forest. He was sure of that. She could still go home, just as she wished. If she returned to the Court of Air later, that was her decision.

"He'll come for me," she promised. Fury rang in her voice, and he'd wager in her eyes as well, though, in his shame, he couldn't quite look at her.

Galen grimaced. "I know."

Sigurd would be furious. He would follow, his retribution fierce, but if Galen and Wren were in the Court of the Forest by then,

Sigurd could come after them without sparking a war. He wouldn't be that foolish, not when he was to blame for ordering Galen to steal Riven's consort, Lia, to begin with.

"Then why?" Wren asked, a crack in her voice that only deepened the ache in his chest.

"Proof of my loyalty to the Forest," Galen replied. "If I give them you, the King of Air's marked mate, they'll have to listen to me."

It would ensure they didn't kill him on sight for daring to return. He would have precious few moments to explain himself, but that would be so much better than the alternative.

Wren wrenched in his grip, letting out a groan of fury. He'd swear he heard her hold back a slight sniffle but still refused to look lest it weaken his resolve.

The ground they stood on was dead and cracked, part of the Unseelie lands that ran in a narrow strip between the Court of the Forest and the Court of Air. Enemy territory. But he was currently an enemy of the Court of the Forest; their wards adjusted to prevent him from shifting directly onto their lands. It was only fitting he tried to enter this way.

Verdant grasses spotted with little flowers lay a step away, but there might as well be a chasm between the two lands. Galen pushed up against the barrier wards of the Court of the Forest, gritting his teeth as they tried to keep him out. He was strong enough to get through, but not without effort, especially given Wren's resistance. He held tight to her as he pushed through the magic, one infinitesimal step at a time.

Finally, Galen broke through the last edge of the wards. The protective ring of magic all but spat him out within the Forest lands, sending him stumbling across the grass and Wren right along after him. She'd yet to speak again, but the feel of her simmering anger at his back was impossible to miss.

Galen sucked in a deep breath, savoring the lively scent of the flowers, the trees, and the richness of the soil. This is where he belonged. His home—the rightness of it wrapped him in its warmth, a balm to anxiety still spiking under his skin.

Wren struggled anew in his grip.

"Be still, Wren," Galen said. "I won't hurt you." But she might well hurt herself if she kept up. It was useless anyway. Her strength of will might be second to none, but human strength paled in comparison to that of the fae—and he was no average fae at that.

She snorted and jerked even harder, demanding his focus.

"You." A female voice cut through the night and caused his heart to skip a heart.

Wren stilled. Gooseflesh rose on Galen's arms. It couldn't be, but he'd know that voice anywhere.

"Sylvie." Galen turned unerringly toward her voice, spotting her at the edge of the tree line. He bit his lip, drawing blood, but there she still stood, the woman of his dreams and the last he expected to see.

But her features lacked all the joy and carefree ease he remembered from their years together. Her face was stoic and cold, giving nothing away—a pure warrior ready for battle. She even dressed like it, her sword free of its sheath and gripped at her side, as if she'd just happened to be on patrol nearby at the very moment he crossed through the barrier.

Fate could be so twisted.

He yearned for her more than all the others, but his betrayal would have cut her deep. Would she listen?

Galen released Wren and took a half step in front of her as Slyvie's attention slid to the human woman at his side.

"What are you doing here?" Sylvie demanded when she glanced back at him.

"I'm free of my oaths to Air. I come to pledge myself to the Forest—to you." His voice cracked over the last part, all the bittersweet emotion he tried to hold back leaking through.

"Who is she?" Sylvie looked past Galen at Wren, who'd yet to utter a word and merely looked around in confusion. "I feel..." Sylvie trailed off.

He knew exactly what she felt. Weeks ago, he could never have expected it either, but so much had changed in so little time. "She bears Sigurd's mark," Galen replied.

Sylvie swore. "One consort to repent for the other?"

Exactly. Galen nodded. "She wishes to return to the human realm."

But Sylvie's expression only soured. Galen's heart clenched, but before he could speak, Sylvie snapped, "Provoking Sigurd will not help the Forest. You bring war to us. You—" Her mouth gaped open. Whatever words she planned to speak were lost.

A prickle of apprehension slid over Galen's skin a moment before he saw a flash of movement from the corner of his eye.

"Fools."

Galen whirled, wide-eyed. His stomach hollowed out. "Katiya."

The Unseelie woman had grabbed Wren in his moment of distraction. She held the frightened human tight against her, a hand over her mouth and sharp claws extended to graze Wren's cheek.

"How?" Sylvie echoed the thought racing through his mind.

The slight tremor of Wren's limbs and her wide-eyed stare were a nightmare come to life. The Unseelie's smirk had the hairs of his arm standing on end. He had not seen Katiya or heard her. Slipping through the barrier should have taken time. Someone should have felt it and noticed. But there she was, where she had not been moments ago. The impossibility of it screamed through his mind. How could she have even found them there?

Sigurd he expected, and soon, but this?

Katiya's clawed fingers drummed on Wren's cheek. "Thank you for the Air king's mate."

Galen lunged toward them with all the speed he could muster, but a second before he reached them, Katiya vanished, taking Wren with her.

Galen collapsed to his knees, letting out a deep bellow into the quiet night. Dread curdled in his stomach as he stared her down the spot where they had just been. All of his plans turned to ash in a moment. Worse, Wren was in danger, and for what? He'd said she'd be safe. He'd...lied, a thing no fae could willingly do. Blood rushed in his ears. His breaths came short and quick. When he glanced up, Sylvie was nearly upon him, sword still at the ready.

End it.

If he were to die, best it be at her hands. But Sylvie slid to a halt a few feet away.

The rush of fear fled as quickly as it came, leaving him numb and hollow.

"Where did she take her?" Sylvie demanded, an edge of hysteria leaking into her voice.

Galen shuddered and pinched his eyes closed. He had no idea—none.

Magic rolled across his skin moments before another voice he recognized demanded, "What is this?"

Galen sucked in a desperate breath before he opened his eyes and hazarded a glance at Ambrose, the gruff Captain of the Guard, where he stood with a number of other fae behind him. Several familiar faces stared at him in shock. Ambrose would have felt his entry and come to investigate, something else he'd anticipated, but in all his musings, Galen never imagined that Wren would have been taken and he'd have to explain himself emptyhanded and while bearing another burden of guilt.

"Galen returned with a human woman," Sylvie said when he failed to respond. "But she was stolen by Katiya, that pink-haired Unseelie woman who ordered our king fired upon."

Galen flinched. He hadn't been there when Riven had taken a poisoned arrow to the chest in defense of his consort, but he'd heard the stories. No court boundaries could keep news like that contained.

Ambrose let out a roar of fury that shook the nearby trees.

"That's not all," Sylvie continued. "She bears—"

An even stronger surge of magic rolled over Galen and silenced the nearby fae. It came from the direction of the Unseelie lands, but it was no Unseelie who bore that magical signature. The power of Sigurd's fury washed over them all like a wave, thick and oppressive.

"Where is she?" Sigurd demanded. "Where is my mate?"

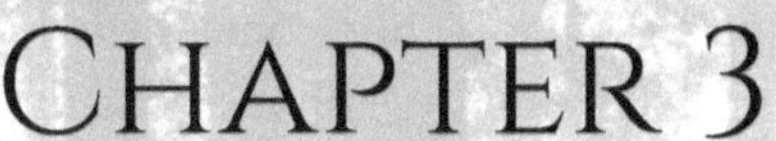

CHAPTER 3

T HE KING OF AIR stood shirtless and barefoot, hair disheveled as if he'd woken in search of his mate and shifted directly there the moment he found her missing. He probably had, following the trail of Galen's magic and the power of the bond Sigurd shared with Wren.

Galen shoved to his feet and steeled his resolve. He couldn't let Sylvie and the others suffer for what he'd done.

"You." Sigurd's accusing stare landed on him. "I felt her here, then—" He snapped his head to the side, looking deeper into the trees from where he loomed just across the boundary line at the edge of the Forest lands. "You've hidden her."

"No, we—" Sylvie began.

"No." Galen put all his strength into that word and stepped in front of Sylvie. "The Unseelie took her."

Sigurd went eerily still. The blue glow of his eyes flared in a corona around him.

"And you what?" he grated out. "Watched? Helped them?"

"No!" Galen yelled. "Never." A traitor he might be, but helping an Unseelie steal a human? A friend? That was the lowest of low.

Air swirled around Sigurd, picking up dust and debris. "How did they get her? Why bring her here?" he demanded.

Other Air court fae shifted in behind him. The tell-tale ripple of magic through the air altered Galen to other members of the Court of the Forest shifting in as well. They had minutes, seconds, until chaos erupted.

"I—" Galen began.

"If the Court of the Forest allied with them to take her..." Sigurd snarled. Wind beat against the barrier between courts.

Galen flicked a half-glance at Sylvie, swallowed, and turned back to the fuming king. "I took her from you and shifted her here."

The wind died. The resulting stillness was more damning and terrifying than the cyclone the king had summoned. "*You* knocked out my guards and stole my mate?"

Knocked out the guards? His brows pinched, but there was no time to ponder that.

"I brought her to the Forest." Galen stood a little straighter, braced for whatever fate awaited him. "But I never planned for her to be in harm's way or for the Unseelie to get her."

Sigurd blinked at him. "She asked you to bring her here?" The pain and doubt in his voice was unmistakable. He truly believed Wren might have chosen to leave, and it gutted him. Sigurd really did love her.

Something about the desperation in his voice hit Galen like a fist to the chest, causing him to flinch. At least he could set the record straight, even if it would damn him.

"No," Galen answered.

The cyclone returned twice as strong. Dark wings sprouted from Sigurd's back as he rose into the center of the torrent. "She cared for you! Pleaded to have your vow to me removed! And this is how you betray her?" The king's voice boomed over the gale. "I should end you for this."

Sigurd advanced, his magical construct slipping through the barrier and hitting Galen with such force that he barely kept his feet. Sylvie shielded her face, hunching forward in an attempt to stay upright. Others let out gasps and cries.

"Sigurd!" Ambrose roared in warning, barely audible above the raging wind storm.

Another wave of magic rolled over Galen from behind, this from a singular source he knew well. The King of the Forest arrived at the worst possible time.

"You dare bring war to my court?" Riven demanded.

Galen hazarded a glance as the King of the Forest strode through the onslaught toward the border, his golden-brown hair whipping in the wind behind him. He hadn't seen Galen yet or chose to ignore him, all his focus on the furious king mere feet away.

Sigurd's cyclone calmed as he floated back to the ground and stared at Riven through the invisible barrier at the edge of the court territory. "You harbor one who stole my mate."

Sigurd pointed to Galen, and Riven followed the angle of his arm until his hard stare made Galen want to sink into the dirt.

Shit. It looked that way, especially with him being on the Forest side, but he hadn't even had the chance to explain himself before everything fell apart.

He had only one chance to get his message across, and he had to make it count. "I am free of my vow to the Court of Air and brought Wren here as a sign of my loyalty to the Forest. To you," Galen said to Riven. His king. "I did not want to betray you or Lia. I care for you both." A truth he was proud to share, even if an outright lie could not pass his tongue. "I belong here, but I was bound to carry out Sigurd's command."

Riven's features remained impassive, giving nothing away. Sigurd huffed air through his nose and crossed his arms. The confession wouldn't earn Galen any favors from Air, but he no longer cared. The Forest was his home, his hope.

"And where is she now?" Riven asked.

Anyone could have answered. Sylvie. Ambrose. Sigurd. Any of the others. They'd heard the truth of it. But no one spoke. The king's question was for Galen and him alone.

So Galen summoned his courage and answered, "Stolen by the Unseelie, by the woman Katiya."

Riven's lips lifted in a snarl. "I felt a human. Here. And a few other places for a brief moment before her presence vanished."

"Impossible," Sigurd snapped, his wings flaring.

It should be. All magic could be felt. A shift. A mark. It would have been how Sigurd found them. He would have followed the magical traces of his mark on Wren to the spot where Galen had taken her.

"A null," Riven said, almost a whisper.

Sigurd reared back but remained silent.

"It would explain much," came Ambrose's acknowledgment to his king.

A null. He'd heard of such a thing, a fae whose magic could not be felt and who could shield others, but it was rare. One had not been reported in generations.

"Chat all you want," Sigurd snapped. "But my mate is missing. She's in danger."

Riven cut him a hard glance. "Now you know how it feels."

Sigurd bared his white teeth. "You knew where she was. You found her in moments."

"*You* had her stolen to begin with!" The ground rumbled, some construct of the Forest King about to break free.

"Stop!" Galen yelled. Both kings turned his way, staring him down as if they might rip him to pieces. "This is what the Unseelie want." The sudden surety of it gave strength to his words and let them flow.

It had been Katiya he'd seen in the shadows on his walk with Wren. It had to have been. She must have knocked out the guards, something he certainly hadn't done. Who else would? She could have followed his shift as easily as Sigurd. It was the only thing that explained how she found them.

But she could have taken Wren earlier. Knocked him out with the guards and taken her then and there. She hadn't. She'd waited, maybe having some inkling of his plan.

"A war between the Forest and Air weakens you both." He spread his arms to encompass both kings. "It only benefits them."

From the corner of his eye, Galen saw Sylvie nod. The simple move bolstered his courage and gave his shaking legs strength to stand in the presence of two monarchs who both considered him a traitor.

"Don't give them what they want," Galen said. "It won't help Wren."

"So concerned about her now?" Sigurd mocked, each word filled with anger.

"Yes. She is my friend." The truth of it spilled out without thought, though the word left a bitter taste on his tongue after what he'd done. "Let me help you save her. Please."

Sigurd crossed his arms and stared him down, his eyes still glowing a bright blue. "And how will you do that?"

"I-I don't know, but I will find a way." He had to atone, to fix things the best he could. In his struggle to prove himself to the Court of the Forest he'd only done more damage, angering both courts and reigniting the threat of war. Even worse, he endangered his friend. She was that, he realized. He'd tried to deny it. It would be easier to part from her that way and to use her for his redemption. But the truth of it couldn't be shut out anymore. Whether she'd consider him thus in the future was doubtful, but for a while there, a bond of trust and comradery had bloomed between them.

Sigurd turned to the fae of his court amassed behind him. "Search for my mate. Now. Leave nothing unchecked." He returned his glowing gaze to Riven. "I trust you'll do the same in your territory?" He stared the other king down in challenge.

"You know how I feel about the Unseelie," Riven responded.

"Do I?" Sigurd cocked one brow.

Galen held his breath, praying for a cease-fire.

"We will search our territory," Riven said at last.

A relieved breath slipped from Galen's lungs, only to catch as Sigurd pointed a damning finger in his direction. "And you will expel this traitor you harbor."

Riven's gaze shifted to him, still cold and impassive. "My court nor I had any part in his plot and offer no sanctuary."

Galen's heart sank—dropped straight through his middle into the endless hole that opened up deep in his stomach. The king may as well have discarded him like dirt off his boots. It wasn't death, but exile to the Unseelie lands could be just as bad...possibly worse. Outside the magic of the Seelie courts, he would weaken. His magic would slowly drain away until it was a husk of its former self, just like the Unseelie lands themselves.

A quick death, like he thought Sylvie about to deliver to him minutes ago, might have been preferable.

"If you let this traitor into your territory while Wren is missing, or if you keep any information about her from me, I'll consider it an act of war," Sigurd replied. Without waiting for a response, he bolted from the ground, spread his wings, and soared over the landscape, no doubt looking for Wren. The guards that had shifted in with him disbursed to carry out his orders.

It hadn't come to war...yet. For that small favor, Galen was grateful.

Riven turned to Galen once more. This time, a hint of sorrow flashed in his green eyes. "You heard Sigurd. You cannot be here while the human is missing."

Galen dropped to one knee. "My king, I—"

With a wave of his hand, Riven silenced him. "I can offer nothing until this matter is resolved."

Strong emotion burned at the corners of Galen's eyes as he raised his head and stared at the king looming above him. He panned his gaze across the familiar faces he'd so longed to see—Sylvie, Ambrose, and other friends in the guard who had come. Each met him with sorrow or resignation.

They wouldn't offer him so much as a word of mercy. They couldn't.

"I understand, my king," Galen replied, his voice hollow as he pushed to his feet.

He turned to Sylvie, trying to say all with a look that he could not with words. Her face was guarded, uncertain at best, but the bob of her throat hinted at an emotion she refused to reveal.

With one last look at the woman he loved, Galen turned, slipped through the barrier, and wandered into the wastes.

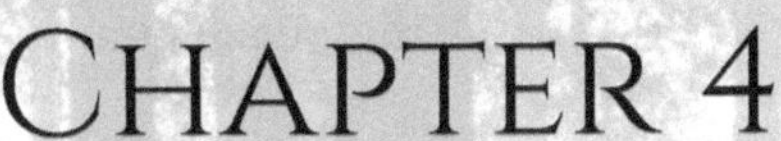

CHAPTER 4

SOMETIME JUST AFTER DAWN, if one could call it that given the cloudy haze that hung over the shadowed lands and obscured much of the light, Galen found shelter in the ruins of what may once have been a small settlement. The half-collapsed stone building wasn't much, but sheltering there would be better than lying out in the open where who knew what might find him. A curved stone still held a little bit of water from a previous rain, though not much. He'd need to find more of it, and food, to be able to survive out here and offer any help in locating and retrieving Wren. More the fool him for not bringing any supplies other than a sack of coins and the dagger strapped to his side, but he had expected his task to be over quickly. And besides, there was nothing in the Court of Air that held value for him—material goods were replaceable, and he had little use for sentiment anyway. But before he could hope to source food and supplies, his body begged for rest.

Inside and out, he ached. He needed to sleep and recover some strength. More than that, though, he prayed the dark oblivion of rest would offer a respite from the horrors playing themselves over and over in his head. What would the Unseelie do to Wren? Some of the abuse they'd brought on humans in the past was unspeakable, and she was at their mercy now thanks to his poor plan and failure. He'd damned her when all she'd ever been to him was kind.

Galen brushed away some dirt and debris with his hands and then sank down on the cool stone floor of the structure. The land was quiet, with few bugs offering up any noise and no noticeable bird sounds—a stark change from what was common in both the lands of Forest and Air. The fresh lively notes he craved were absent from the air. Instead, all that reach him were scents of dust and decay.

With a sigh, he stretched out on the floor and stared at the ramshackle roof above. He'd never had a knack for building things, but it seemed stable enough, at least for a few hours of rest.

He'd nearly drifted off when the sounds of crunching dry grass shoved away the haze of sleep. Galen sat bolt upright and silently slid his dagger from its sheathe. He focused in on the sound, the steady pace that someone or something took as they drew near his hiding place. Whatever it was made too much noise to be a small creature, this was something larger.

Galen shifted into a crouch on the balls of his feet and edged toward one wall bearing a few cracks. He peered through the largest, pulse racing as he squinted at the bit of tall, yellowed grass he could see beyond a large fallen stone that had once belonged to a neighboring structure. Nothing presented itself, but the sound continued. The creature was almost upon him now, likely lured by his scent. Galen adjusted his grip and moved silently toward the entrance to his little shelter.

Unseelie creatures could be wicked—more fierce and blood-thirsty than many of those found in the Seelie courts. They had to be to survive in such a place.

He sucked in a deep breath and readied himself to plunge the dagger into whatever stepped through the narrow archway.

Something stepped heavily just on the other side of the wall. The hint of a shadow fell across the doorway. *Any second now...*

"Galen?"

His entire body stilled. The shock of that voice nearly sent him pitching forward toward the door. It couldn't be. *A hallucination. It must be.*

A blonde head poked into the space and swiveled in his direction.

"Woah!" Sylvie stepped into the room, her hands raised and open.

"Sylvie," he gasped.

Her head cocked to the side, the hint of a smile pulling on her lips. "Expecting someone else?"

"You—" Galen stammered. "I could have killed you. I nearly..." His arm holding the blade fell slack at his side.

"But you didn't." Sylvie lowered her hands. "Good thing I thought to call out, huh?"

"Why are you here?" His mouth still hung agape, his mind trying to wrap around the reality that she was truly there, in front of him, in the Unseelie lands.

She shrugged. "I thought you might need some things?"

Finally, he noticed the pack on her back, an extra sword hilt sticking out its top. Not just any blade. It was the sword he'd left in his quarters within the Court of the Forest. He'd recognize those leather bindings—ones he crafted himself—anywhere.

"You didn't seem to have much with you," she continued.

"I—"

Galen could only blink, speechless, as she lowered the pack and set it on the ground with a heavy thump. No wonder she'd made so much noise in the brush. The thing must weigh a good deal.

"The king sent you?" Galen guessed. "Ambrose?"

The joy slipped from her features as she shook her head side-to-side. "No. I came on my own."

Galen's chest hollowed out. "You need to go back. Now. Right now. I won't let you get in trouble because of me." He'd caused enough trouble. Dragging Sylvie into it? Unthinkable.

"I'm already here," she replied in her carefree tone, as if she brought snacks to the training yard rather than supplies to an outcast and traitor.

"But if anyone finds out, you could be punished." He couldn't have that on his conscious too. Not Sylvie. He wanted to be with her again more than anything, but not here, not like this.

"Rivenean promised that the Court of the Forest would not shelter me."

"They're not," she snapped. "You're in the Unseelie lands. I chose to walk out here with some supplies in tow and managed to run into you." She shrugged again as if her actions were of no consequence. "The Court of the Forest has taken no action, only me."

"But you—" He jerked his head to the side. "I won't let you get in trouble because of me."

"Oh hush," she scolded him with her lips pursed and brows pinched. "I can make my own choices."

Galen opened his mouth to speak again, but the piercing look she shot him had his jaw snapping shut.

"It's already done," she continued. "Besides, I hauled this stuff all the way out here. You could at least say thank you." Sylvie plopped down beside the bag, crossed her arms, and stared up at him with her accusing look that always made him wither.

Galen raked a hand through his hair with a sigh. "You're right. I'm sorry. I'm very grateful that you brought things for me. To take such a risk is..." *Stupid. Foolish. Ridiculous.* He pinched his eyes shut. She'd risked so much for him, so much more than he deserved. "I'm honored you would do that for me," he said at last.

When he peeked his eyes open again, Sylvie smiled up at him. "You'd do the same for me."

He would. That and so much more. He'd give his life for hers if the situation called for it.

"I'm so thankful for what you've done, but you should—"

"No," she interjected. "Let me stop you there."

Once again she had him on his heels and standing a little straighter.

"I'm staying. For the moment, anyway. So why not save yourself some trouble and just be grateful?"

Galen ran a hand down his face. There was no arguing with her when she set her mind to something. Fine. He'd drop it for now, but that didn't mean he was comfortable with the risks she took. Far from it.

"I am grateful," he said at last. "More than words."

"Good." She nodded, leaving no doubt the matter was closed, at least in her mind.

"So..." he started, settling on the floor, the bag between them. "How did you find me out here?" True, he'd taken few measures to hide his trail, especially at first. Honestly, he'd done little more than put one foot in front of the other on an aimless quest until he spied the ruins. Then, he'd approached with caution lest he stumbled upon wild creatures, or worse, Unseelie.

"It wasn't too hard to follow your scent. After all, there aren't many Seelie out here. Plus"—she pulled a necklace from within her shirt—"I had a little help." A hint of color touched her cheeks as she held it up, a golden leaf—twin to the one on his earring—dangling from its length.

She'd used its magic to find him. He should have known. Warmth stirred in his chest, and he fought the urge to rub at it. The leaves were a pair bound as one, enchanted so that the owner of one could always touch it and feel a pull toward its other half. Sylvie had given him one, not a year past and kept the other for herself. It was his most valuable possession, his treasure, one he wore at all times.

"Anyhow," she said, tucking the necklace away and glancing at nothing to the side, her cheeks still flushed, "I saw which direction you went, so that helped, too. But first, I shifted home and gathered a few things I thought you might need."

And to give the others time to disburse, no doubt. If anyone had seen her or knew what she planned, surely they would have tried to stop her—brave, reckless woman.

Sylvie tugged open the ties on the bag, letting the opening fall slack. The sword slid toward him. Its weight nudged the top further open, revealing some of the items inside.

"It's not much." She gestured to the pack. "Just some simple food, water, a change of clothes."

Galen reached for the sword, his fingertips ghosting over the hilt.

"Oh, that." Sylvie tucked some hair behind her ears and refused to quite look at him. "After everything that happened with Lia, I, um...took a few things from your room that I...hoped you might need again someday. They sent the rest of your things to your parents, I believe." She winced, looking back at them. "Sorry for that."

Galen's father had sent a brief letter not long after he'd arrived in the Court of Air. The man had been proud of him—*proud* that he'd betrayed the King of the Forest. The thought of that note—one he'd quickly burned—still left a bitterness at the back of his throat he never could cleanse. By right, he should report his father, though he hadn't actively worked against the Forest in some time, and Galen was fairly sure Riven knew of his father's true loyalties yet let him remain in his territory anyway. Whether his parents had received his things, they didn't say, but his Father had given him leave of a family home and funds they still possessed in the Court of Air, things he accepted only because he needed them.

"Thank you. This means a lot to me," he said, trying to block out all thoughts of his treasonous father and his quiet mother, who always seemed to look the other way where her husband's dealings were concerned.

"I knew how much you liked that blade," Sylvie replied.

Galen shook his head. "Not just the sword. Thinking of me then after what I'd done then, being here now... I don't deserve it." He hung his head, unable to quite look at her.

"You do," she said softly. "Lia told me that Sigurd had an oath from you and that you didn't want to do it. Besides, I know you. Deep in my heart, I knew you wouldn't do such a thing without reason. Though, I wish you'd just come back once you could and not dragged Wren into it." She leaned back, her palms flat on the floor, staring at him as if she were trying to work out a puzzle.

Me too. "I didn't think anyone would listen unless I brought some kind of proof of my loyalty."

"You doubt us so much?"

Dim light filtered through the doorway and cracks in the structure, but it was more than enough for him to see her clearly, to make out every shape and shadow of her form. Sylvie looked the same as he remembered, his petite warrior with her shimmering hair that liked to escape its ties and curl around her ears. Her eyes still held that sparkle of mirth and wonder, even on such a dark and desperate day. She didn't hate him. Didn't doubt him. That alone had a tingling of desire racing under his skin.

Still, he'd never felt more a fool than he did today. Galen had been so certain of a cold reception, perhaps a deadly one. That Sylvie would believe him even after what he'd done, that she would put herself at risk to help him, was such a rare and wondrous thing that he hadn't let himself believe it possible. That kind of hope, if crushed, could destroy him.

"I had no idea it'd be you who found me first," he replied, refusing to speak the truth that he *had* doubted, even if it was done in defense of his heart. "Not everyone would be so lenient."

"No." Her gaze dropped to the floor. "I suppose not. It was pure luck that I did. Fate." She reached for her shirt, bunching up the material where he guessed the necklace rested below. "I'd been out on patrol, keeping busy, and you happened to pop to mind. So, I touched the necklace. One moment the pull was so faint, just like it had been since you'd been gone, and then, suddenly, it wasn't. It was so close to me." A smile stretched across her lips as she gazed back up at him and pushed another wayward lock of hair behind her ear. "I thought it might be a trick or some fault in the necklace, but I shifted toward it, and there you were."

"There I was," he echoed. He could still scarcely believe it himself. Fate had been on his side in that, perhaps, though it had turned around and damned him with the loss of Wren.

Sylvie pushed off the floor and sat up straighter. "Galen..." she started. Her features shifted and pinched as she seemed to consider her next words. A pink tongue slipped over her lips, the sight stirring desire low in Galen's center.

"Yes?" his voice cracked through his dry throat.

Once, she had been his rival, then his friend. But over time, that friendship was no longer enough. He craved something more, something deeper. It wasn't just about sex and mating, though he couldn't deceive himself if he tried to say he didn't want that too, but most of all, it was about trust and connection. That unbreakable bond he'd never shared with anyone, not even kin. So many times, he'd almost worked up the courage to spill his desire to her, but the fear of losing her, of breaking the beautiful thing they already had, held him back.

After his betrayal, the most he hoped for was to see her again. That alone was a gift, one he'd been given. Yet even now, his foolish heart couldn't help but yearn for more.

"I..." Sylvie leaned in ever so slowly.

Galen held his breath, fearful of breaking the moment.

"I should let you get some rest." She pushed off the floor in a rush.

Galen fought to hide his disappointment as she went about hastily dusting off her pants.

"You look exhausted," she continued. "When was the last time you slept?"

He rubbed the back of his neck. "It's been a while..." He'd managed little rest the night before the final competition and none since.

"Right. Well, I'll stand watch and alert you if there's any trouble." Sylvie bolted for the door.

"But—" He reached for her.

She twisted around on her toes and wagged a finger at him. "Rest. Then we can talk more." With a wink, she turned and vacated the space beyond his outstretched hand.

CHAPTER 5

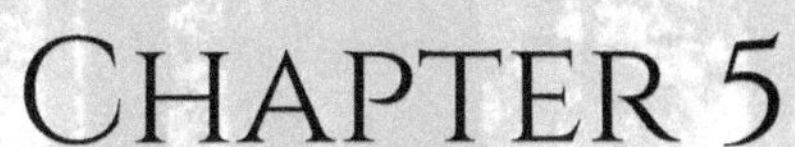

WITH SYLVIE ON WATCH, Galen managed to rest. Her nearness threw a shadow over the towering mountain of worry and regret that had taken shape within him over the past hours. Shortly after he woke, Sylvie left quickly to return to the Court of the Forest with a plan to return. It was a bittersweet and quick parting, but a necessary one. Every moment she spent with him was another that risked her future. He'd considered telling her to stay away—for her benefit, but in the end, he couldn't quite bring himself to. Not yet.

The day passed slowly, time dripping by like honey instead of water. Galen forced himself out of the shelter and back toward the area where he'd shifted to with Wren, just outside the Forest lands. If he was going to find anything useful, he'd wager it would be there. As much as he longed for Sylvie, even more so, the driving need to somehow help his friend pushed him on like a strong wind at his back.

When that effort turned fruitless, Galen crouched amid strands of tall, brown grass. Their brittle stalks gave way with ease, and it took absolute stillness not to disturb them as he waited for something...anything. It'd been years since he was a trainee, and had been forced to do such exercises to build his skill. His body let him know it, too, muscle groaning in pain and a tingling numbness building in his feet if he stayed too long in one spot. Perhaps it was foolish to linger and let time slip away, but some inner sense told him to remain there.

As the cloudy sky darkened toward night, Galen prepared to leave, the weight of his failure an added burden, when he spotted something on a rise some distance away. Multiple figures moved on the horizon, dark forms against the muted and hazy sunset. One had antlers or some other feature reaching from their head into the sky. The fine hairs on the back of his neck rose. *Unseelie.* But why there, and for what cause?

It was too small a party to attempt anything against the Court of the Forest unless there were many others near that he could not see or sense. Another appeared from nowhere, though he could not see or sense the magic of their shift—an even rarer ability among the Unseelie given the fade of their magic. Something that might be a tail flicked out behind the newcomer. The small group of others joined them. A moment later and they were all gone, shifted away.

He swallowed heavily. If he'd been seen, they could outnumber him easily.

Galen waited in absolute stillness for a few minutes, pulse racing and poised on the tip of his toes and ready to spring should the Unseelie appear around him.

But no threats presented themselves, nor did they return to the low hilltop or any other place he could see. Convinced they were gone, Galen shifted to the spot where the Unseelie had been. Their scent lingered faintly in the air—they hadn't been there long.

The top of the hill was wide and flat, an ideal perch for taking in the surrounding territory. Much of it was covered by shorter prickly grass, brown and dry like much of the surrounding land, but a section of the center was nothing but dirt. A chill crept down Galen's spine as he advanced on the dusty plain. Marks and symbols were worked into the ground, though not ones he recognized. His brows pinched as he stared at them, trying to make sense of what they could mean. Nothing leaped to mind, but there was a hint of familiarity that he couldn't quite ignore. A bit of magic clung to the space, too—the faint feeling of something evoked by the working.

As he pondered the oddity, another form of magic rolled across his skin, this one signaling a member of the Court of the Forest shifting in close behind him. Galen turned, his momentary apprehension slipping away as he beheld Sylvie at the edge of the rise. He breathed a sigh of relief and felt the corners of his lips rise as he beheld her. She'd returned, just as she said. He knew her words for truth, and wouldn't have doubted her anyway, but there was always the possibility that someone could have observed her actions and forced her to remain in the Court of the Forest. The possibility had nagged at him all day.

Sylvie released the pendant of her necklace, obviously having used it to find him again, and made her way toward him.

"Sorry it took me a while to return," she called.

That was the last thing on Galen's mind at the moment—he'd have waited years if he had to. Besides, at least she looked refreshed. Hopefully she'd taken time to rest herself. "Come and have a look at this." He gestured to the ground in front of him.

Sylvie cocked her head to the side as she came to a halt next to him and peered at the workings. Her lips pursed together. "So strange. I feel like I should be able to read it or know what it means, but I can't."

"I had the same reaction." Galen rubbed the back of his neck as he stared at it once more. "It's Unseelie, I believe. I saw a few of them up here before they shifted away, and I came to investigate."

"Shifted?" Sylvie stared at him, her lips still parted.

"Rare. I know." He nodded.

"Could it be Katiya again?" Sylvie planted a hand on her hip. "She's caused us much trouble lately."

He wondered the same. The lack of a ruler, the beating heart of the Unseelie magic, had not only drained the life from the Unseelie lands, but also the power of its people. Most, that they knew of, had little in the way of real magic, instead relying on brute force to scratch out a living among their Shadowlands. "It's possible,"

Galen replied. "I thought I saw one with a tail, but I was too far away to be sure."

Galen dropped into a crouch and stared at the designs. The soil was still pebbly around the edges as if someone had just dug the symbols into the ground and left the excess dirt along the sides of the swirls and loops. The wind had not smoothed it out, nor rain. "This has to be new," Galen said. "Has anyone reported something like this?"

Sylvie dropped into a crouch next to him. She reached a hand toward the designs before drawing it back. "You're right. And no, not that I have heard."

They shared a look, all the implications of what such a design could mean sinking in.

"A honing point," Sylvie said, speaking the fear taking root at the tip of Galen's spine.

He nodded slowly. "They would need such a thing to bring groups of them here, or to leave in mass once more." Thoughts flowed between them with ease, all focus on the mission at hand. So easily they slipped back into their years of training and comradery, like donning a favorite outfit and reveling in how well it fit.

"An invasion?" Sylvie gave further voice to his growing worry.

"Possibly." Galen stood in one smooth movement. Sylvie followed. "Or they still have Wren and wish to make a show of it." He assumed Sylvie would have told him if she'd been found. Her silence on the matter spoke volumes, and none of it good.

She swallowed thickly. "I need to report this right away."

The Unseelie could return at any moment, a troop of them, and whether they brought Wren with them or not, that was something that the Court of the Forest needed to know...and the Court of Air.

"Go."

Sylvie gave a short nod. "I'll come back. We'll need to watch this spot, and I can volunteer for that since I'll be reporting it."

"I'll meet you here," Galen replied. Already he dreaded what came next. The Court of the Forest might pass on word to the

Court of Air, but if he was going to begin making up for his mistake, if he had a chance to somehow help Wren, the Court of Air needed to know this information and quickly. It would be a huge risk going back there, but he owed it to Wren to try.

"See you—" *Soon.* That's what he'd meant to say, but the word slipped away as Sylvie grabbed his hand and gave it a little squeeze. Truly, they didn't need words. They never had. Against the odds and despite what he'd done, they'd been reunited. They would be again. He had to believe that.

"Be safe." She smiled and then was gone.

Galen shifted to the border of the Court of Air. He stepped across the line, expecting the wards to have been altered to hold him back and keep him—a traitor—from the territory, but he slipped right through.

He blinked in shock, taking in the change of scent and scenery that assailed him. Then, a low hollowness spread out in his chest, reminding him of exactly why such a standard step had been missed. The King of Air was so worried about his missing mate he hadn't had time to think of the protections for his court.

He loved her. The bastard truly did. Only that could explain it. For all his faults, Sigurd was a careful ruler who cared for his court. The Court of Air grew stronger under his reign—happy, unified. Galen might hate it there, but even he couldn't deny that. Yet, the king neglected his duty for the sake of one human woman.

Somehow, that fact made Galen respect him more. If Sylvie were missing and in the hands of the enemy, he would have the same single-minded focus on her return—he had once when she was in danger from Unseelie invaders. All thought, all concern for himself, had fled his mind at the thought of her in danger, and they didn't even share a mark—a mating bond.

As he stood inhaling the pine-tinged breeze, no members of the Court of Air shifted in to arrest or execute him. If they were still searching for Wren, as they must be, guards would be coming and going through the wards frequently. His presence was likely just a raindrop amid the torrent.

A humorless laugh crawled up his throat. It should be a blessing, but at that moment, it was an ironic inconvenience. He needed attention to relay his message, but not enough to get him imprisoned or killed on sight.

Galen stepped back out of the territory and into the Unseelie lands. Already his senses mourned the loss of fresh air and life that filled the Seelie courts and the subtle liveliness of magic that flowed through his veins while he resided there. He was weaker in the Unseelie lands but not without any magic.

When Galen first took his vow to Sigurd all those years ago, Sigurd taught him a spell to summon one of his many eagles. After all, if he might be called upon to spy for the King of Air, they would need a way to communicate that didn't involve either of them leaving their respective courts. The birds were the messengers, stealing secrets across court boundaries. An animal passing through the wards of a court was a normal thing, not one felt like a fae crossing might be.

Galen used that spell now. It was one he'd hoped to be rid of, to no longer need, but the years of memorization and practice came easily as he released his magic into the soft breeze.

The summons complete, Galen set about crafting a message for the bird to deliver. Sylvie hadn't included paper or writing utensils in the pack of supplies she'd brought him. And why would she? But the pack itself was made of leather, with several decorative straps that could be lost without compromising its integrity. Galen used his dagger to cut free a strip of leather and then carefully scratched his message into its surface.

He sat on the ground for long minutes after he completed the missive, rubbing the edge of the leather strip and waiting for an eagle to respond to his summons. All the while, Sylvie raced through his thoughts, as she often did. Had she been successful in her mission? Would she be waiting for him when he returned? As much as he yearned for it, it would be better for her to stay far away. Though just the thought had his chest growing tight and his shoulders hunching inward.

Finally, he spotted a speck in the sky heading his way. Galen rose to his feet and dusted off his pants as the bird made its final approach.

"Took you a while," Galen remarked as a stately, brown and white eagle settled upon the ground and tucked in its wings.

The damnable thing had the gall to look annoyed as it stared up at him and tilted its head to the side.

"Take this to your master as fast as you can." He bent over, offering the strip of leather to the eagle. *And don't you dare lose it.* They hadn't lost his messages in the past, none that he knew of anyway, but with his current luck, this would be the time the bird would let the message slip.

The eagle cawed at him before taking the leather and bolting back into the sky.

Galen had done his part. The rest was up to the messenger bird...and Sigurd.

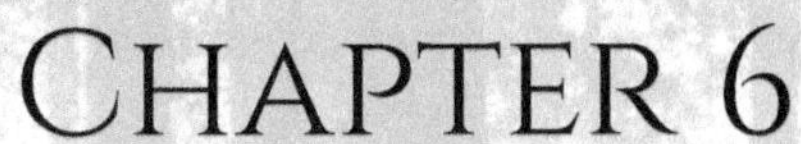

CHAPTER 6

F ULL DARK HAD FALLEN by the time Galen returned to the site of the Unseelie honing point. Little moonlight crept through the blanket of clouds in the sky. A weariness pressed down on him that had little to do with exhaustion. The Unseelie planned something, likely involving Wren, given their recent capture of her not too far from the honing point they created. If she had come to harm, it would be his fault and his alone, a burden he wasn't quite sure he could bear. Besides, that would certainly spell his permanent exile or death. Compromising an innocent human, one mated to the King of Air? What had he been thinking?

Selfish thoughts. That's what. And look where that led him.

Fate was strangely kind to reunite him with Sylvie, and yet, what had he done with that time? Nothing important. He hadn't spoken any one of the dozens of confessions that had raced through his mind while they'd been apart and that he'd planned to tell her the moment he saw her again.

Just like always, he hesitated. He waited. But damn if he wasn't running out of time—time that he'd endangered Wren for. He couldn't let that be for nothing.

Galen pinched the little golden leaf dangling from his ear between his fingers. Instantly, he felt a strong pull toward a formation of rocks not far away. His lips curved up in one corner. She'd returned and found a clever watch post, if a bit obvious. Even so, it would give them the vantage they needed to see if the Unseelie returned.

Galen took some time wandering in the wrong direction before changing course and creeping stealthily toward Sylvie's hiding place. If anyone else was watching, he didn't want to give away her hiding spot or, worse, the fact that she consorted with a traitor.

"Took you a while," Sylvie whispered as he advanced the last few feet on her location. "I was beginning to think you returned to that broken old building I found you in."

Galen dropped into a crouch near where she sat. From this position, the rocks guarded them on most sides, but an empty space between two boulders provided an advantageous view of the nearby short hill.

"Now, why would I do that when you're here?"

Sylvie sat a little straighter. Her lips parted.

A sudden flush crept to the back of Galen's neck. *Damn.* He hadn't meant that to sound quite like it did. Or did he? It might be their last night together if the sinking feeling in his gut was correct. Why shouldn't he just tell her right that minute?

But as he gazed at her still form bathed in the dim blue moonlight filtering through the clouds, the answer hit him like a smack in the face. If by some miracle she returned his affection, he couldn't let her become an outcast too. He wouldn't risk her trying to slip out to visit him in whatever poor excuse of a life he could muster in the Unseelie Shadowlands. Neither could he make their parting harder by giving her hope of something that could never be. That burden was his alone. He'd become a traitor—to two courts and his friend. He didn't *deserve* the woman he loved.

Galen shifted on his feet and pulled in a deep, steadying breath. "Anyhow," he continued in an effort to change the topic. "What news did you learn?"

Sylvie blinked, and the momentary look she had vanished. In an instant, she slipped back into her role as a member of the elite guard as easily as breathing. Once again, they were just filling their roles, just partners on a mission. Sylvie stared through the gap between the rocks before responding. "There was mostly agreement with the suggestion that the Unseelie may be planning to return to this spot soon. Others thought it may be a distraction." She shrugged. "There's only one way to find out, though. The Court of the Forest has posted sentries here and in other places near the border where we've seen activity in the recent past." Sylvie glanced at Galen. "I assume you went to the Court of Air?"

He settled down onto the parched and lumpy soil. "To the border, to relay the same message."

"And they listened to you?" She tilted her head to the side.

"We'll see. I sent the message by bird."

"By..." She mouthed the second word. "Is that how you did it? How you spied for him?"

The rocky ground was suddenly far more uncomfortable than it had been moments ago. And just like that, the conversation wandered to a place he didn't want it to go. "Part of it," Galen admitted, his shoulders slumping.

Sylvie bobbed her head. "I wondered. I knew it had to be something since I couldn't remember you being gone much unless you were on patrol or some other assignment for the Forest."

"Have there been any updates on Wren?" Galen couldn't quite meet Sylvie's gaze as he asked. Instead, he focused on the little rocks near him and plucked up a smooth one to rub between his fingers.

"Nothing," she replied. "We reported to the Court of Air that there was no indication of her in the Forest, and they reported likewise."

Galen swallowed the tightness in his throat. It was too much to hope for good news, but at least the two courts were communicating. That was something.

"Get some rest," Sylvie said, drawing his attention back to her, where she once again peered through the rocks toward the hill. "It may be a long night, and who knows what morning will bring."

The order made sense. He *needed* rest, but that was the last thing on his mind. Sleeping away possibly his last hours with her seemed such a terrible waste. "I can take the first watch," he offered instead. And second, third, whatever it took.

Sylvie cut him a sideways look and rolled her eyes. "I can tell you're not yourself. Rest. It will help. Besides, I rested earlier today. I'd wager you haven't."

Galen set his jaw, ready to argue.

"Do it for me," she continued quickly.

The request slipped right between his ribs and planted itself in his heart.

"Then I can rest later while you take watch, and I won't have to worry about you falling asleep on me." She winked.

Galen huffed a breath through his nose. "Like I would."

"Did you forget our training already? Always be prepared. Take precautions. Don't make foolish assumptions." She wagged a finger, whispering the last part in a deep, gruff voice that could only be an impression of Ambrose.

"What if I have?" he teased.

She rolled her eyes again. "You're better than that. The Galen I know would never slack off on his duties."

Just betray his king, his friend, a little voice whispered in the back of his mind. All the humor died from his expression.

"Sleep." Sylvie pointed at the ground. "Or at least try to."

"Fine," he mumbled before digging around in his pack for the blanket Sylvie had thought to stow there for him. It wasn't much, but it would be a better pillow than a rock.

CHAPTER 7

S OMETIME IN THE MIDDLE of the dark hours of the night, Galen woke. For a blessed moment, he forgot where he was and why. A rock dug into his side, and all he could think was that he'd rolled out of bed and onto something. But then, he blinked against the darkness and saw Sylvie sitting just where he'd left her, peering out between the rocks, and everything rushed back. Galen barely stifled a groan as he pushed off the hard ground.

"You're awake. Good," Sylvie whispered.

"Any change?" he asked, though he already knew the answer. If there had been, she would have woken him.

"Nothing." Sylvie turned away from the rocks to face him fully. "Though I did feel a strong presence earlier, from above." She pointed toward the dark, cloud-strewn night sky.

"Sigurd?" Galen asked. Few in the Court of Air could summon wings like his to drift among the clouds. Even some Unseelie they'd spotted with winged features seemed to lack the ability to fly for more than short distances.

"Possibly," Sylvie replied.

He still searched for Wren then. Did he ever stop to sleep? To rest?

"He cares for her that much? This human, Wren?"

"Yes," Galen replied. "I believe he truly does."

Sylvie tsked and shook her head. "She must not know all of what he's done."

"All? No, I'm sure not. But she knows enough. I told her as much."

She sat a little straighter. "And yet she bore his mark."

Galen sighed. "She did." Wren was smart, strong, and brave. Whatever she saw in the King of Air, he couldn't quite understand. But somewhere within him, she'd found something to admire, to love possibly.

"Let's switch." Galen offered Sylvie the rolled-up blanket. "It's your turn to rest."

Quiet as they could, the two switched spots, though Sylvie didn't lay down, just sat with the blanket in her lap next to Galen.

"You like Wren, right? Not just because she's human, but something about her?" Sylvie asked.

"Not the way Sigurd does," Galen replied quickly before Sylvie could get the wrong idea. "I met her in the competition. I wanted to be free of my vow to Sigurd, and that was the fastest way I could think to do it. She wanted something similar, to go home." From the corner of his eye, he saw Sylvie nod along. Galen turned toward her. "Actually, she reminded me a lot of you."

"Of me?" She sat a little straighter.

Galen nodded. "Brave. Kind. Strong-willed. We were allies in several of the rounds. I suppose, by the end, I thought of her as a friend."

"Like me," Sylvie said.

Without thinking, he reached out and took her hand in his. She gave a sharp inhale of breath but didn't pull away.

"No. No one could mean as much to me as you."

Her lips parted as she blinked at him in return. "Galen." His name was barely a whisper on the gentle breeze.

Shit. And there he went, stirring up things he planned to keep to himself. It had always been so easy to hide his feelings until now. "You're my best friend," he amended. "Closer than my family."

Sylvie's expression settled into something he couldn't read, but she squeezed his hand in return. "As you are mine."

She pulled her hand from his and used it to tuck some hair behind her ear before tugging the rolled blanket close.

Sylvie looked away to stare at the boulders in front of them. "Unlike Wren, I could never love someone like that, though," she whispered.

Galen's chest tightened. She might as well have said she could never love him, not after what he'd done.

"It has to be more than just physical fulfillment and lust for a mark to settle, doesn't it?" she mused. "Sigurd is fair to look at, but what could she have seen beyond that to stir such feelings?"

Whatever they had did go beyond the physical—he could see that in the way Wren looked at Sigurd and in her faith that he would keep his word to her, to do as she asked in granting the wishes of the other finalists, including his. Somewhere beyond all his vile sins, she'd found something to cling to.

If only he could be so lucky.

"He did seem a bit different with her," Galen replied, thinking back to that night at the finalists' ball. "I didn't see them together often, but when I did, their connection was impossible to miss, even before she accepted his mark." Sigurd had stared at Wren like she was the moon, sun, and stars. It was so obvious to anyone who dared to look, except perhaps to Wren herself. The words had come so easily to Galen's lips as he watched Sigurd stare at Wren. *"He's in love with you."* How Wren was the focus of such attention and couldn't see it herself then, he still couldn't understand.

"Perhaps love changes people." Sylvie adjusted her position, and Galen sucked in a breath as she moved ever so slightly closer to him. It was probably an accident or something done without thought, but he couldn't miss it, not when their legs nearly brushed. "Maybe he saw something in Wren that brought out the good in him?"

"Maybe," Galen echoed. If so, Wren was the one to see it. But... Sigurd had kept his word. He had revoked his vow without thought or question. It was a risk to him and his reign. He had to know that Galen would try to return to the Forest and would almost certainly tell them everything he knew about Sigurd, his court, and his plans—not that Galen had the opportunity to do that yet.

He might never get that chance after what he'd done taking Wren, but Sigurd couldn't have possibly considered such an outcome when he removed the vow. If he had, he'd have struck Galen dead instead.

"And whatever she saw was enough to forgive him for his past, or at least let her look past it," Sylvie surmised.

"You think it's so easy to forgive?" Galen asked.

"When love is involved."

That wayward bit of hair had slipped over her pointed ear again, and she moved to push it back, grazing Galen's sleeve in the process. That little touch, so incidental and meaningless, had his whole body clenching tighter. The scent of her all around him, like new budding roses, didn't help matters.

"After all," Sylvie continued once her hand settled atop the blanket roll once more, "Look at Rivenean and Lia. The way he betrayed her by endangering her sister was a terrible thing. In some ways, I understand why, but it doesn't lessen the vileness of the act. Yet still, she loved him enough to see past that, to forgive him, as did the court. And me. And you, I suspect." Her head cocked to the side, a small smile pulling at her lips. "Why else would you try to swear loyalty to him again unless you forgave him?"

For you. The words curled on his tongue, ready to be spoken, but he held them back. She was right, though, too. Galen's years of loathing for the vow Sigurd demanded of him soiled any sense of loyalty or love he could have for that king long before Sigurd first called on Galen to spy for him. Riven, however, he'd admired and respected. Galen had pledged his service to him and been as loyal and forthright as he could possibly be given his previous vow to Sigurd. Day after day, he saw how the king loved his people and tried to do his best for them, even when he fell short or when he was seen as less than his father—still a young king trying to fill large footsteps. Galen would have laid down his life for the King of the Forest. He loved him in his way. And though he'd learned of the terrible ploy he'd constructed and felt that hurt and betrayal deep in his heart, he still found reason to wish to remain in his service and at his side.

Rivenean had made a terrible mistake and taken it too far before he could repent. His plan had gone array before he could bring it to the conclusion he'd been so sure would follow.

Bitter laughter caught in Galen's throat, and he stared at the ground. "I think I understand him even more now. He tried to do what he thought would help his people, but he failed."

"Lia saw that," Sylvie said. "It hurt. It gave her great pain. But her love was enough to forgive him and move forward."

Sylvie's hand settled on his leg, and Galen nearly jolted out of his skin. His head snapped toward her.

"I think you tried to do something similar with Wren. Well, it may not have been best for the Court of Air, but you never meant her harm. She wanted to go home. You knew the Court of the Forest would keep her safe and see to her wishes."

"But then everything fell apart." His gaze drifted to her hand, still on his leg.

"We all make mistakes. Miscalculations. The ability to see the future is one of the rarest, and even then it can mislead."

Only once had he met a fae with that ability, and very recently at that. Galen's thoughts drifted to Lysandir, the prince of the Court of Fire, as he lifted his gaze to Sylvie once more. He'd seen something the day they met, though if it had anything to do with Galen, Lysander had never said. Could he have foreseen this outcome? But no, Lysandir liked Wren as well. If he'd seen her in danger, surely he would have warned her if no one else.

"You're lost in thought." Sylvie withdrew her hand, and Galen nearly groaned at the sudden ache of loss that filled him.

"Kings are easier to love and forgive than simple guards like me," he replied.

"I don't know about that." Sylvie unfurled the blanket and pulled it around her shoulders. The night had grown chill, though it was hard to feel cold when her nearness had him burning up from within.

"Kings come with a lot of expectations," Sylvie said, tugging the blanket tighter. "They're held to a higher standard, and everything they do is seen and judged by those around them. That goes for anyone who wants to love them too. To love a monarch is to take on all of their burdens as well, and as we both know, those can be many. I..." She trailed off, looking away. "I've never had aspirations for that. I always wanted something..." She paused, her lips twisting to the side before she gave one short nod. "Honest and true."

Galen bit his lip so as not to smirk at the response. *Honest and true, huh?* That ruled out a traitor like him immediately. "And have you found someone like that?"

Ancients help him if she had. Asking the question alone invited more pain, but he couldn't help it.

"You'd like to know?" She glanced at him meaningfully, but damn if he could make out whatever she tried to convey.

"I would."

Breath caught in his throat as Sylvie slid closer, her body brushing up against his. Every hair on his body stood on end. She stared at him, and for a brief and beautiful moment, Galen thought she might lean in to kiss him. Instead, she snuggled up against his side and laid her head on his shoulder. "Then I'll tell you someday."

"Someday?" he gaped, still trying to reconcile the fact that she rested against him. It wasn't the first time. They'd shared warmth and companionship on many a night during their years together in the elite guard, often leaning on one for support or comfort, but somehow this felt different. Maybe it was the adrenaline coursing through his veins, the letdown of a hopeful kiss vanishing into the night, or just the past days catching up with him. Any way around it, it still took a full minute before he could make his body relax against hers.

"Why not now?" Galen asked once he regained his composure.

She made a non-committal sound as he felt her shoulder brush against his. "I don't think it's the right moment yet."

Not the right moment? How could it not be when it might be one of their last? Galen sighed heavily and tucked his arms closer to his body.

"Are you cold?" Sylvie lifted her head. "Here, let's share the blanket."

Before he could protest, she flung part of the material around him, cocooning them in together before she laid her head on his shoulder once more. "Wake me if anything happens, and don't you dare fall asleep on watch."

A huff of laughter caught in his throat. As if he could possibly sleep with her resting against him.

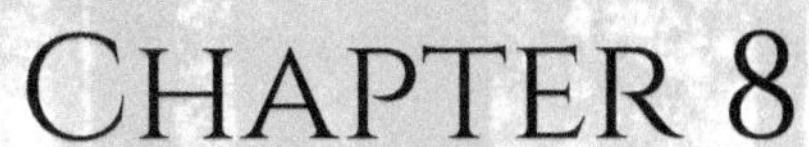

CHAPTER 8

D AWN LIGHTENED THE SKY beyond the clouds, harkening another dreary day in the Shadowlands. Not long after Sylvie had fallen asleep, Galen eased her down until her head rested on his thigh. It relieved the numbness in his arm and was certainly more comfortable for her but infinitely more distracting for him. Sylvie's head in his lap? *Idiot.* He berated himself for the hundredth time, slowly shaking his head as he gazed at her sleeping form. With how easily she slept, one might think him the most comfortable pillow imaginable, but he was far from that.

Galen sighed and glanced back through the opening in the rocks and confirmed that there was still no activity on the rise. The night had been eerily quiet and devoid of action, as if the whole land held its breath, waiting for something to happen.

Perhaps he'd been wrong in his suspicions. There were any number of reasons the Unseelie might try to create a honing point, if that's even what it was. It had to be his guilt making him think it had something to do with Wren.

Galen turned his attention back to Sylvie. For hours, he'd resisted the urge to run his fingers along her hair or maybe dare to touch her slightly parted lips. Her presence was a constant call beckoning to him, one he'd barely been able to resist thus far.

When he'd envisioned his ideal outcome upon his return to the Forest, Galen had planned to waste no time before confessing his love to her—assuming her reception of him was anything above icy. He'd lost her once, and the thought of wasting any more time pining in silence, as he had for years, rather than pursuing what he wanted, was ridiculous to him. Now that she was here, though, now that his plans had gone awry, everything was so much harder.

He dared to touch a tangle of blond hair that had escaped her braid and floated just above her cheek. The strands were silky against his skin—lovely.

Magic rippled across his skin, one wave then another, over and over. Galen jerked his hand back and snapped his attention toward the hill. It was empty, as it had been, but the feel of the magic was undeniable. Many fae had shifted into the area nearby—strong ones.

Sylvie jolted, shoving herself off him and blinking rapidly as she woke. "I felt—"

"Me too," Galen replied in a harsh whisper.

Quietly, he took to his feet, ignoring the ache and tingling of sitting still in the same position for too long. Galen went entirely still as he spotted the source of the magic over a boulder to his right. A mass of fae baring the colors of the Court of Air gathered in a field not too far away. One among the rest was unmistakable from his imposing presence alone—Sigurd, King of Air.

Galen swallowed the knot in his throat and shrunk out of their view. It was a war party, their purpose unclear.

"Shit," Sylvie muttered at his side as she caught sight of what drew him still and silent. "Do you think they expect the Unseelie?"

"I hope so." The alternative, that they might be preparing an assault on the Court of the Forest or some other ill ploy, made him queasy. One thing was clear, they weren't just there to talk, not with a force of that size and dressed in armor.

More members of the Court of Air arrived, the magical impact of their arrival charging the air around them.

"I need to warn the King." Sylvie met his gaze, her features solemn.

"Let one of the others go." She wouldn't be the only one watching this spot. Whoever else was assigned nearby would have felt such a large group arrive, too.

"Galen..."

"We don't know what they plan. Don't rush away just yet." *Stay with me.* He wanted to beg. If she left now, that might be it. The Court of the Forest could order her to stay there or post her somewhere far from his reach.

Her lips pursed, but she nodded. "You're right."

Hopefully.

Galen and Sylvie peeked from their hiding spot toward the group from the Court of Air. The fae filed into ranks, much of their attention poised toward the hill with the strange symbols. So, they'd gotten his message and chose to listen. Though such a force seemed like an overreaction unless they knew something more that the Court of the Forest—or at least Sylvie and Galen—did.

They didn't have to wait long before another wave of magic washed across them, this one awkward and dissonant, raising the hairs at the back of Galen's neck. He didn't need to glance at the hilltop to know Unseelie had appeared. But when he did, he gasped. At their front stood a fae he recognized, Katiya, and in her grip... "Wren."

His stomach bottomed out. There could be no mistaking it. Though Wren stood, he couldn't tell if she was hurt.

"Now I have to go," Sylvie said, never tearing her wide eyes from the group of Unseelie. Though a smaller force than the host from the Court of Air, it was the most Galen had ever seen together. He'd wager the same was true of Sylvie.

Galen gave a jerking nod before grabbing her hand and clenching it tight. "Be safe."

The Court of Air wouldn't trifle with the feel of one member of the Forest shifting away. In the wake of this sudden appearance, they might not feel her at all.

Sylvie squeezed his hand in return before dropping it. "You too."

And then she was gone.

Galen didn't have the chance to mourn her absence before Sigurd's pained roar cut through the quiet morning. "Wren!"

Galen lurched back to stare through the opening.

An Unseelie with long white hair stepped forward from Katiya and Wren. "King of Air." His deep voice boomed across the plane. "I believe I have someone you'll want returned. Let us discuss terms."

Galen nearly snorted. As if the Sigurd or the Court of Air would be willing to have some calm discussion while they still held Wren. He watched as Sigurd and his Captain of the Guard, Moria, advanced alone on the Unseelie. Katiya, Wren, and the white-haired male moved to meet them.

One of Galen's brows arched up. Perhaps someone had knocked some sense into the King of Air. It was unlike him not to fly into a fury. Galen had expected him to charge in, sword raised, a display of magic at hand, and an army at his back. He certainly dressed for it with his winged helm—the figure he cut in his armor was one of terror from the skies. But eerie calm seemed to shroud him instead.

Perhaps love really could change someone.

The two groups met, a few sword lengths of distance still separating them. Some discussion took place, but through Galen strained his ears, he couldn't make it out.

Please come to some agreement. Let Wren go free. It was a fool's hope, but all he had to offer as he watched in silence, waiting for something to happen.

Every muscle in his body stiffened as Katiya pulled Wren back toward the Unseelie. "No. Damnit!" He slammed his hand on a rock. Moria, too, retreated to the host of Air, leaving Sigurd facing the lone Unseelie warrior.

The two men drew swords, and Galen scowled at the scene. *A duel? Seriously?* What could one Unseelie hope to do against the King of Air? That had to be good news for Wren, though. For once, he was grateful for all of Sigurd's arrogance and power. Win the fight quickly. Get Wren back. Be done with it. Then she would be safe from the mess Galen dragged her into.

Galen found Wren again where she stood next to Katiya, likely locked in her grip. But from what he could make out at a distance, she didn't seem relieved—the opposite. His brows pinched. Surely she knew Sigurd's power.

The distant clang of metal rang out, Sigurd and the Unseelie meeting in a show of swordplay. The two appeared evenly matched, meeting one another blow for blow, but that shouldn't be possible. "Why drag it out?" Galen mumbled. There was no need to put on a show. If given the chance to fight, Galen wouldn't hesitate to finish the farce as quickly as possible and free Wren, and she wasn't even his mate.

Tiny fingers of cold dread crawled around his chest and wormed their way inside as he watched.

With one fierce blow from his sword, the pale-haired stranger knocked Sigurd back, earning cheers from the group of Unseelie gathered on the hilltop. Galen's stomach bottomed out, and he swayed on his feet. It wasn't a farce. That single Unseelie was as strong as the King of Air.

"Impossible," he whispered to himself. The ground rumbled, shaking the rock formation which Galen peered through. He leaped back, grabbing his pack before one of the larger stones tumbled off to land where he'd been standing. Where the two men fought, the ground had split wide, forming a small gorge where one had not existed moments ago.

That power didn't come from Sigurd.

Without another thought, Galen strapped his sword to his back and prepared for the worst.

This was no normal Unseelie. They should have such power, especially not of the magical sort. Their magic had faded with their land, fled with the death of the last Unseelie king when his magic did not settle on an heir.

Galen's heart stuttered as a possible solution slid into place within his mind. The whole world seemed to tilt on its axis as he watched the Unseelie male use his impressive sword to literally cut through Sigurd's volleys of wind that the King of Air sent rushing toward his opponent.

This was not a fight between a Seelie king and some random Unseelie. Two kings fought this duel, and the King of Air was losing.

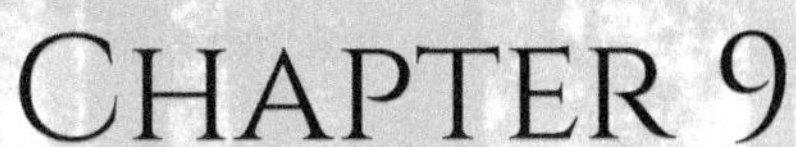

CHAPTER 9

"**S**HIT." GALEN SNAPPED HIS attention to Wren. There was no way Sigurd would simply leave her with the Unseelie unless he was certain he could win, but that likelihood faded with each passing moment. What would happen to her if Sigurd lost? Galen's fist clenched at his side. They wouldn't let her go free. A human was too valuable.

I have to do something. I have to help her.

No one else moved to intervene, likely afraid of interrupting the duel. But what did he have to lose? Galen was an exile already—condemned. The least he could do was try to atone for his mistake of dragging Wren into this in the first place by getting her out again.

He just needed the right moment...

Galen crept quickly through the tall grasses toward the group of Unseelie. With all eyes on the dueling kings, no one bothered to look his way, but he stayed low to disguise his approach all the same. Wren and Katiya were partway down the slope, ahead of the group at their back, still cheering on their fighter.

He saw Wren mouth something, which caused Katiya to snarl rip her hand away. A smear of red coated Wren's arm. *Shit.* His heart kicked against his ribs. She'd been hurt.

There had to be a way to get her out of there, and quickly.

Wren cried out, her full focus on the duel at hand rather than whatever wound was on her body. Galen twisted toward the duel, a resounding gasp floating across the plane as Sigurd crashed to the ground and tumbled like a ball across the dead and dying land. His torn and bloody wings vanish.

A quick glance at the Unseelie showed all eyes on the kings. If Galen were to make a move, that was the moment.

Without another thought, Galen shifted to Wren and wrapped an arm around her middle, pulling her close. Katiya screeched and lunged their way, but not before Galen initiated another shift. A heartbeat later, they stood some distance away, staring at the hill they'd just vacated. A gasp tore from Galen's throat as other forms shifted in around the Unseelie, these bearing the colors and armor of the Court of the Forest.

Sylvie. Always his mind went to her.

Wren shoved against him. "Get off—"

"Don't panic."

"Galen?" Instantly, she stopped struggling.

With her calm and away from the Unseelie, Galen loosened his hold. Wren twisted toward him, her mouth agape. Something about her fortitude in the face of this nightmare warmed him. The hint of a smile twitched at the corner of her lips. "I couldn't leave you with them."

She shook her head, chest rising and falling with heavy breaths, but the look on her face was easy to read as writing in a book—relief.

Finally, she—

A screech cracked through the air only a few feet away. Galen's attention jumped past Wren to where Katiya had appeared, two short swords dawn and her face full of raging fury.

Galen shoved Wren behind him and stepped between her and the Unseelie. He wasn't about to let them take her back. Not now. Never. Galen unsheathed his sword and adjusted his grip, staring down his foe across the rocky ground punctuated with shoots of browned grasses.

"How dare you!" Katiya raced toward him, blades raised and ready to strike.

He raised his blade just in time to catch the brunt of her strike as the swords crashed down into his. Galen stepped back, steadying himself against the impact ringing up his arms. Given her lithe form, Galen hadn't expected such strength despite the Unseelie predilection toward physical strength.

Galen shoved Katiya's blades away with a grunt and realigned his stance, following her movements and anticipating the next strike.

Behind him, he heard Wren scramble across the ground.

Good. Hopefully, she could flee and get out of harm's way. If Katiya tried to go for her again, he'd stop her.

Katiya struck once more, and again Galen blocked her. As she leaped back and recovered, he spared half a second to scan the hilltop. The Unseelie stared down the guards from the Court of the Forest, neither side advancing or engaged, nor did it seem any tried to slip away.

A furious screech escaped Katiya as she jumped to the side and then attacked from a different angle. Galen was too slow to react, missing any projection of her planned move in his distraction. The tip of one blade cut through his tunic and into his bicep, stinging like a searing flame down his arm.

Galen gasped in pain as he stumbled back and tried to adjust his grip. He gritted his teeth as he clutched the hilt of his sword with both hands. Of course she had to injure his dominant arm.

A golden glow seeped from Katiya's eyes, illuminating the vicious smirk twisted on her lips. "Trying to undo your crime?" she taunted. "It's far too late for that."

Galen snarled and rushed at her, trying to catch her off guard, but she anticipated his move and blocked him easily. Again, they met in a clash of blades, Galen's injury roaring with the punishing force of her strikes.

A tornado erupted in the background, swirling up from the ground and consuming the two kings. Galen tried to ignore it as he blocked another blow from Katiya, but the sight of a woman rushing toward the chaos nearly stopped his heart cold.

"Wren!" he called for her, but she didn't turn, possibly didn't hear him over the roar of the wind given her human senses.

Of all the damnable places for her to rush toward.

"Fool." Katiya rushed him. Her lead blade clashed with his, and he shoved her away, the motion sending them stumbling in opposite directions, but not before her second blade caught the back of his calf and cut deep.

Galen let out a cry of pain and fell to his knees. He shoved against the ground, trying to rise, but the leg wouldn't support him. Katiya sauntered toward him, twisting one blade in a playful show. "It's too bad," she smirked. "When I end you, you won't see the greatness in store for the Unseelie court."

His pulse hammered in his chest. Sweat slid down his skin as possibilities raced through his head. His could still shift—maybe—but then no one would stop Katiya from retaking Wren.

I need... He searched the fae from the Court of the Forest with his eyes as he ignored the rest of Katiya's taunts. The little golden leaf dangling from one ear was suddenly heavy. He couldn't die, not without seeing Sylvie again, not without confessing everything to her.

And if he died now, he wasn't sure he could rely on the others to keep Wren safe. They hadn't jumped to protect her like he had—hadn't shifted her away. Perhaps in the chaos, they didn't even notice her.

"Oh well," Katiya sighed. She was right in front of him now, barely a sword-length away. Blood painted her nails and the tips of her fingers on one hand—Wren's blood. "So be it."

Galen raised his sword, a last show of defense, but his injured arm had nothing left. He wouldn't be able to block her again. Katiya raised her blades, ready to strike.

CHAPTER 10

IT WAS NOW OR never. Shift or die. Galen reached for the magic tingling under his skin, ready to set it free, when a familiar feeling washed over him, and a new form appeared just to the side and in front of him.

Katiya's blades crash down, but they never reach him. Galen stared wide-eyed at the blade that took the blows, held by the most beautiful sight imaginable.

"Stay away from him." Sylvie flung Katiya's blades back, sending her stumbling a few steps at the unexpected intrusion.

"Sylvie." Galen nearly choked on her name, a sob of mixed relief and terror catching in his throat. For the briefest moment, he thought he envisioned her in his last moment, her golden hair somehow bright under the cloudy sky as she stood resplendent in her full armor—which she hadn't been wearing when she left him minutes ago.

But she was real. When he needed her most, she came. Again.

Katiya jumped back with a frustrated cry, putting space between herself and Sylvie, who stepped in front of Galen.

Tears burned at the corners of his eyes, but he hastily blinked them away. There was no time for emotion, not when the woman he loved faced down the foe that nearly ended him.

Sylvie's presence gave him a burst of strength, her spirit burning through him like a crackling flame that warmed rather than consumed.

"Another of the Forest King's guards. How quaint," Katiya replied. "As if either of you have a chance against me."

Galen pushed himself upright, keeping all weight off the injured leg that still roared in agony. He could do little with his injuries, but he'd be damned before he cowered and left Sylvie to fight alone.

"You saved me," Galen said to Sylvie, but he kept his gaze focused on Katiya, where she paced in a tight line a few feet away, eyeing them up and down and forming a new plan of attack, her tail swishing behind her.

"I always will," Sylvie replied, her attention, too, focused on their foe.

That single phrase empowered him, cloaking the pain that tried to consume him.

While his enemy still paced and waited to strike, Galen spared a quick glance for Wren. Still free, still on her feet, and still advancing on the magical construct of wind that blocked her way to the king she loved. Sigurd must have done it to keep her away from harm. It might have worked if she wasn't so persistent.

When he glanced back to Katiya, she also watched the human woman.

"Eyes over here," Galen snapped, raising his blade in a shaking hand.

She bared her fangs. "You can barely hold your sword."

But hold it, he would.

"You—" Katiya started, but stilled as more members of the Court of the Forest appeared around her, one with their blade poised at her throat.

Galen's eyes widened. She wouldn't dare pose a threat to Wren now.

"*You're* severely outnumbered," Sylvie taunted, advancing on her. "Still wish to fight?" She lifted her blade, the point poised toward Katiya's face. "Drop your weapons."

Katiya snarled but did as commanded, her gaze flicking toward the tornado surrounding the dueling kings.

"She can shift," Galen warned. "Don't let her flee."

A Forest guard surprised him by reacting immediately and grabbing one of Katiya's arms. Sylvie sheathed her sword and took the other. Their magic should be strong enough to hold her, even if Katiya tried to flee. That she hadn't yet was a wonder, but as he watched her twist her head toward her surrounded comrades, he understood why. She didn't want to leave them.

Even the Unseelie had a sense of honor among them.

A wave of magic tingled across his skin. The familiar feel called to him, causing his chest to clench tight. He turned in the direction it came from and watched as the magical twister split apart, the debris falling from the sky to reveal the two kings bound in vines and another, the one whose magic he'd felt, standing among them.

Rivenean. Galen swallowed the tightness in his throat.

Wren shoved herself up from the ground where she must have fallen and raced toward Sigurd. Her cries carried over the new, eerie silence. The collective fae seemed to hold their breath, waiting to see what would happen next.

Galen thrust the tip of his sword into the ground and leaned on the pommel for support. It'd be bad for the blade, but that was the least of his worries. It could be sharpened. He, on the other hand, might bleed out before he ever saw what the kings might do when three of them faced each other down on the plane of battle.

Blood seeped from Galen's wounds. Pain burned down to his bones. The world around him grew blurred at the edges. It would only be a matter of time before he passed out, or worse. He needed healing. But as an outcast, who would offer that? He couldn't do it, nor Sylvie.

As if his thoughts drew her attention, Sylvie slid her gaze away from the kings and toward him. Her eyes widened, a green glow seeping from them. "Where's a healer?" she snapped to the other guards around her.

The nearby guards who'd come to assist looked between one another. "Waiting at the border," one said.

"Get one." Sylvie pointed at him. "Now. Supplies too."

"Right away," he replied, the words still hanging in the air as he shifted away.

Moments later, he reappeared with Leigh, another member of the elite guard who Galen knew well. Her eyes widened as they landed on him. "Galen," Leigh gaped.

Despite the pain in his body, he nearly flinched at that look and braced himself for rejection. She knew what he'd done, that he was an exile, a traitor.

"He's injured," Sylvie commanded. "He needs healing."

"Right." The shock faded from Leigh's features as she advanced on him.

Galen's good leg wobbled precariously, and he slid to the ground, his knee hitting hard on the rocky soil.

Leigh knelt before him and granted him a tight smile. "I bet you have quite the tale to tell."

He grimaced, unable to form a reply.

"Another time," she said. Her hand landed on his shoulder in a friendly pat just before her eyes slid shut. Magic rushed out from her form, sliding through Galen in a tingling rush as it sought out his injuries and knit them together.

Immediately, the cool burn of the magic brought relief to his aching body. Galen sighed, slumping further onto the ground as the worst of his wounds were tended by Leigh's magic.

At some point, his eyes had slid closed as he savored her healing touch. When he opened them, Leigh still knelt before him, her arm folded across her knee instead of clasping his shoulder.

"I fixed the worst of it, but I have to save some magic in case—" She gestured around them.

Galen nodded. Things could still come to blows at any moment, and then she'd have others to tend. "Thank you for healing me after I—"

She shook her head. "I don't know all of what happened, but we saw you fight the Unseelie and help the human." She gave him a light poke. "I think I'll see you again soon."

Leigh helped him to his feet. "Until then, rest, and use this." She passed him one of the small leather bags that had been tied to her waist. "And get away from here. You're in no shape to fight anymore today."

And go where? He kept the bitter retort to himself. He could stumble back to the rocky outcropping and retrieve the pack of supplies. Maybe shift back to the little hovel he'd rested in the other night. Galen picked up his sword and sheathed it, its weight somehow a comforting presence.

"I'll take him somewhere to rest."

Galen's heart lurched against his ribs at Sylvie's proclamation.

"Switch with me," she said to Leigh.

Heart in his throat, Galen watched as Leigh took Sylvie's place, keeping a tight hold on the still scowling Katiya, though the Unseelie woman's focus was glued to the trio of kings.

"Take her to the others and keep a hold of her until Rivenean decides what's to be done. She can shift," Sylvie added.

"I'll see it done," Leigh promised with a sharp nod of her dark head.

"I can't go back to the Forest." *Yet.* That unspoken word was too much of a hope, too uncertain to speak aloud.

"*You* freed Wren," Sylvie stopped directly in front of him. "Without you, she may still be in their clutches. They would still have leverage to use against us and our king."

Galen shook his head, swallowing the lump of emotion that formed at her words. "She freed herself. I just got her away and gave her the chance to run." His gaze drifted over to the trio of kings, where Wren stood beside a bound and bleeding Sigurd. She had the chance to flee, but she chose not to use it. Even so, she should be safe now. Whatever happened with the kings, Riven had the upper hand, and he wouldn't let her come to harm. Deep within him, he knew that to be true.

"Let's get you somewhere to rest."

Before he could protest, Sylvie grabbed his hand and shifted them both. Galen wobbled, his injured leg still stinging as they appeared near the rocky outcropping. Sylvie released him just long enough to grab the bag of supplies and their cast-aside blanket before taking his hand once more. Galen sent out his magic to touch hers, planning to aid in the shift, but she snapped her hand away.

"Don't you dare," Sylvie snapped, scowling at him. "Save your strength. That's an order."

"Giving me commands now?" Galen asked. A hint of mirth crept into his tone as he took her in. For some reason, he loved it when she scowled or ordered him around. Sylvie was never one to guard her emotions, showing everything on her face and speaking her thoughts as soon as they came. It didn't matter that he'd nearly died or that war might still break out at any moment. Alone, just the two of them, even for a moment, brought him joy, especially when she acted so much like the woman he'd known for years despite all that had just occurred.

"And you better listen to them." She wagged a finger at him before gripping the wrist of his uninjured arm, her fingers digging in hard enough to cause him to wince.

"As you wish," he replied.

She huffed, and then they were slipping in a blink from one place to another. The walls of the half-crumbling shelter he'd discovered took shape around them, the ceiling so Galen could touch it if he lifted his hands above his head. Little bits of muted sunlight flowed in from the cracked walls and open doorway, their sudden appearance stirring up bits of dust and dirt that drifted through the air.

Sylvie dropped his hand as if it burned her and turned her back on him. The sudden cold shoulder had Galen standing a little straighter. If she turned and left without a word, it would gut him, even if he couldn't fault her for spending as little time with a traitor as possible. Others saw her shift him away. They would expect her to return immediately, not linger with the likes of him.

But before she could leave, he had to tell her the words bouncing on the tip of his tongue. "Thank you for—"

"How dare you!" She whirled on him, eyes blazing with a green glow.

Galen held his hands up in front of him and stepped back. "What—"

"You almost got yourself killed!" she screeched, uncaring if anyone or anything lingered nearby to hear her. "If I'd been a second later, she could have killed you! That close, and poof—" She snapped her fingers. "You'd have been gone. Just like that. Right in front of me!"

It was then he noticed the sheen of tears in her eyes. One little droplet fell free to drip down her face as she pinched her eyes closed.

Shit. Now he'd gone and made this strong woman cry. She hadn't known he meant to shift away, or at least try to. Would she have stepped in to help him if she did? *Yes.* He knew that to be true the moment the doubt slipped into his mind. Of course she would. She always did.

"I planned to shift—" he began.

"You planned to?" She flung out her arms in exasperation. "Waited a little late, didn't you? And how have those plans turned out recently?"

He flinched against the verbal. Sylvie grimaced, seeming to regret her words, but she'd already hit home. Her pointed barb had him on his heels, the need to defend himself rising up unchecked.

"What about you?" he snapped in return. "You shifted in and engaged the enemy directly. A risky move. Far too risky." One they'd been taught never to do. A second or two late or a bit off in the shift could have dire consequences. "Not to mention that you're here engaging with me instead of back at the battle. They know you helped me. That can't be good for you, helping a traitor."

Sylvie's lips quivered before smoothing into a thin line as she held her head a little higher. "I couldn't not help. I couldn't watch you die."

"Why?" Galen pushed. "Why risk yourself for someone like me?"

She shoved hard against his chest, sending him stumbling back a step. "Because I love you, you idiot!"

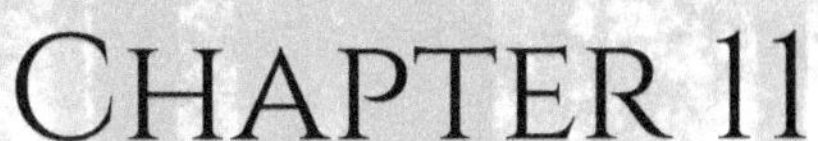

CHAPTER 11

GALEN'S HEART SKIPPED A beat. The confession echoed in the silence of the small room. Sylvie stared at him wide-eyed, mouth slightly agape, her chest rising and falling with heavy breaths.

Those simple, powerful words broke the chains that had bound his truths for so long. All hesitation and fear of rejection vanished.

Galen moved directly in front of her. Sylvie's breaths ghosted across his skin as she stared up at him, unspeaking.

"I love you too."

And then his lips were crashing into hers. Galen's arms wound around her body, his fingers tangling through the ends of her braided hair as he tugged her close, heedless of his injuries. They didn't matter. Nothing did, except showing her exactly how much he loved her, too. A thousand feelings sparked under his skin as her soft lips pressed back against his. Sylvie's breath filled his lungs, his soul. He'd imagined the moment for years. Dreamed of it. Yearned for it. Yet all his many imaginings couldn't compare to the real thing, to the feel of her against him sharing his passion despite the blood and dirt that marred him.

Her palms found his chest, the material of his shirt bunching in her fingers as they dug toward his skin. And then she shoved him, hard, breaking their kiss and sending him stumbling back until he hit the wall, little bits of dust and debris floating down atop him.

"Sylvie—"

But once again, she cut him off. "You love me?" she asked, her voice caught somewhere between a screech and an uncertain question.

"Yes." Galen's chest rose and fell as he reclined against the wall, still reeling from the kiss and her sudden rebuff. "I love you, Sylvie. I have for years. You. Only you."

Of all the ways she could have reacted, she laughed. Not a simple chuckle, but a deep thing that shook her whole body. Sylvie's hands covered her face, and when she pulled them away, new tears streaked down her cheeks. Galen stood frozen in place, mouth gape, able to do nothing but stare at her as various emotions chased themselves within.

Sylvie dropped to sit on the floor, still rocking and shaking with a mix of laughter and tears. "Then how dare you?" She rubbed at her tear-stained face, staring up at Galen where he still clung to the wall in shock.

Galen shucked the weight of his sword, letting the scabbard clatter to the ground. His dagger belt too. He approached her slowly, like a spooked horse ready to buck and flee, one hand up and open in front of him to show that he meant no harm. Her hard stare never waivered as he settled on the ground near her. "How dare I what?" he finally asked, his voice barely a whisper.

"Not tell me. About your vow to Sigurd. The spying. Everything. How could you just leave me in the dark and then...leave? You left me."

The pain etched on her face would have brought him to his knees if he didn't already sit on the ground. "I had to leave. It wasn't a choice."

"You still could have told me."

"That I was a traitor?" Saying the word aloud was painful. Confessing it to her if he didn't have to? Impossible. "That I was forced to betray *our* king when I didn't want to? How could I have ever put that burden on you?" Either she would have had to turn him in or become a traitor with him by keeping his secrets. The first he hoped to avoid. The second, he could never allow.

"We could have worked something out together." She sniffed. "Come up with a plan, some way out of it."

And just like he feared, she would have kept his secrets. "It was bad enough I had to betray our king. I couldn't risk you getting wrapped into that too. I never wanted you to be hurt because of what I had to do. My faults, my errors."

She opened her mouth to speak, but this time, he cut her off. "Even right now, you could be implicating yourself. They saw you shift me away. They may notice you did not return. Plus, you brought me supplies, stayed with me, helped me—*me*, an exile and a traitor." His voice rose of the word, a burning fury inflaming his thoughts at the risks she took. "Every moment you spend with me risks yourself and your position. I couldn't bear it if anything were to happen to you or you were punished because of me."

"Then you know exactly how I feel," she snapped before crossing her arms and hugging them close to her chest.

"How you feel?" He gaped, sitting a little straighter.

"Yes. How *I* feel." She huffed, tossing her head so her braid slipped back over her shoulder. "It tore me up inside when you left. When I thought I'd lost you forever. All I could think was that I should have known somehow and kept you out of trouble. The male I've loved for years committed this horrible act and vanished before me, and I *knew* it wasn't like you. I *knew* you must have been forced. But what could I do?" She smashed her fist onto the ground. "Absolutely nothing."

Galen could do no more than blink in the wake of her words. Of everything, one line stood out among the rest. "You've loved me for years?"

Sylvie pursed her lips and looked away. "Honestly, how did you not figure it out? All this time—"

The beginning of a laugh caught in his throat. "I've loved you for years too, Sylvie." Saying it now was so easy, so right.

Her head snapped back in his direction.

A sheepish smile touched his lips at her wide-eyed look. "Possibly longer than you've loved me. But I was afraid of losing you.

If I confessed and you didn't feel the same, it might have ruined things between us, and I couldn't risk that. I'd have rather have had you as just my friend forever than lose you completely. And once I did lose you, when there was a chance I might never see you again, or you wouldn't want to see me after what I'd done, I realized how much of a fool I'd been. I should have told you years ago; consequences be damned. I…" His throat closed up as he regarded her, the softening of her features, the slight wobble to her lips. "I robbed us of the years we might have had, and now it's too late. I'm a traitor to not one but two courts. An outcast. I have nothing to offer you, and I can't let you throw away your life for me."

She deserved better. It might kill him to send her away, but she couldn't stay with him, not as he was. She had a life in the Forest. Friends, family, a respected position. It was her home and where she belonged, to say nothing of her magic and how the renewed vibrance of the Court would help it flourish, enhancing her powers and extending her life beyond what she might have in the Shadowlands. Here, her magic would slowly drain away until it was a husk of itself like the dying land. She would exist—for a time, but existence cut off from the Seelie Courts was unpleasant and so much shorter than it might otherwise be.

"You still don't get it." She wiped at her eyes. "That loss you felt? I feel it too. Everyday. I'd rather be banished with you than suffer a life of emptiness."

No. No! His inner voice screamed through his mind. He shook his head. That was the opposite of what he wanted.

She seemed to catch the wild look in his eyes and leaned toward him with her palms on the ground, so near to him that her arms brushed his legs and her scent swarmed him.

"When have I ever not gone after something I wanted?" she asked.

Never. She'd always put her full heart into everything. The top of their training class. The first to get promoted. It frustrated him to no end at first, until one day, it didn't. The competitiveness he felt toward her shifted into something like admiration. Why be her rival when they could be allies? Why struggle against one another when they could combine forces and put everyone else to shame? And so, a tentative alliance had formed, then a friendship, and then... He wasn't quite sure the moment it happened, but soon, he couldn't imagine life without her at his side.

Her head tilted to the side, her braid falling forward, the end of it teasing him through his clothes. "You really think I'll back down now when I know you want me too?" Her voice was hoarse and breathy. An enhancing verdant glow spilled from her eyes, showing all the emotion coursing through her.

But she wasn't the only one who glowed with strong emotion in that moment, his aqua light met hers in the narrow space between them, and something in Galen snapped.

He lurched onto his knees, lingering pain be damned, and cupped her face in his hands. Sylvie gasped as he drew her close, until their noses touched and barely any space remained between their lips as they shared the same breath.

"No," he said at last, the roughness of his voice surprising him. "I don't think you will. And when have I not cleaved to what you wanted?"

"Right now," she whispered.

"Don't you know I'd give you anything?" And then his lips were on hers again, as fierce and hungry as before.

But where before she'd pulled away, this time, Sylvie groaned against him, leaning into the kiss and meeting him with such passion it made his head swim. She rose on her knees to meet him. Their chests pressed tightly together as her arms round around his neck, and her fingers slipped through his hair to pull him closer. Tentatively, Galen teased her lips with his tongue, only to be met with strength and enthusiasm that nearly knocked him senseless. He didn't think then, couldn't, as he took all that she had to give and met her as an equal match. It's messy, feverish, overeager—too many desires pent up for too long spilling out in one single kiss.

CHAPTER 12

A T SOME POINT, THEY ended up on the floor, Sylvie underneath him, her strong thighs wrapping around Galen's hips and tugging him closer until he was helpless but to buck against her warmth, eager to be closer, to feel her skin against his, and claim a priceless treasure he thought long gone. Sylvie's leg slid down his. Her booted foot grazed the wicked wound on his calf.

Galen hissed in pain, jerking his head up from hers. Leigh's magic had closed his wounds, but they were still inflamed and tender, waiting for time to heal what magic had not finished.

"Your wound," Sylvie gasped. She all but scurried away from him, sliding back along the ground. "I'm so sorry. I should have been more careful."

"It's okay," he gritted out, aching from both the injury and the loss of her. Galen reached for Sylvie. "Please. Don't pull away. Don't stop," he all but begged. "Not now."

"But you're..." Her gaze drifted to his leg, then settled slightly higher. Her eyes widened as she caught sight of the evidence of his arousal straining against his pants. Her pink tongue slipped out to coast over her lips.

"We could try again without those boots." His gaze raked her in return, her heavy breaths, her flushed cheeks, and the tangled mess he'd already made of her hair. "Or the rest of it," he added before he could lose his nerve.

Galen didn't wait for her reply before reaching for his shirt and hauling it over his head. He unlaced his boots with a fury before kicking them off and standing once more to work at his pants. The entire time, he was acutely aware of Sylvie's eyes glued to him and the deepening of the flush on her cheeks as he worked loose his belt, then the laces, and finally pushed the fabric free, taking his underthings with it. The glow of her eyes flared as his manhood sprung free, flush and ready.

He swallowed the tightness in his throat as he waited for her to speak, to move, to do anything but stare at him in hungry silence like a predator waiting to pounce. He'd gladly be her prey. Galen rolled his shoulders back, refusing to hide himself from her in even the smallest way. The time for modesty, for hiding his desires, was long gone. Let her drink her fill and take her time. The way she looked at him alone was worth it, stirring desire deep in his abdomen that had his cock twitching in eagerness, a bead of precum already leaking from the tip.

She licked her lips again before snapping into a flurry of movement, pulling at the ties and bindings on her armor and shucking it faster than he could have believed possible. Each piece gone was a reward, from her bare feet wiggling on the stone floor to the toned muscle of her bare arms.

Galen's abdomen clenched when she finally pulled off the top portion of her underthings, revealing the pert, dusky nipples on her perfect, small breasts. Sylvie bit her lip and hastened to remove her bottoms. She hadn't quite looked at him the entire time—too focused on her task or from some other emotion, he couldn't say.

He groaned as the last of her clothing slipped free, revealing the thatch of fine blond hair between her legs. Galen palmed his length without thinking. His cock jerked against his hand, yearning for her touch, wondering how she would finally feel wrapped around him.

A deep flush stole across Sylvie's cheeks as she kicked away the last of her clothes and glanced up at him under her eyelashes. Hastily, she tugged her braid over one shoulder, letting it conceal much of one breast before covering her most intimate part with one hand. Her throat bobbed as she watched him in silence, not quite meeting him full-on.

"So shy," he mused. "It's not like I haven't seen you naked before. I believe we've shared many a stream and changed before each other countless times." He cocked a brow at her, suddenly emboldened by her momentary burst of modesty.

"That was different," she whispered, backing up a step or two until she hit the stone wall and jolted forward with a slight gasp.

In the past, it had been in the line of duty—cleaning after a battle or while on patrol, a quick change after a difficult day of training. He'd caught more than a glimpse of her naked form over the years, though he'd always tried to give her and their fellow guards privacy.

"It was," he agreed, stalking toward her. "But I..." He planted a palm against the cool stone wall before leaning in to hover just in front of her. "I don't want us to hide from each other anymore."

"What if I'm not—" She stuttered. "What if you don't like..." Her gaze flicked quickly down her form and then back up to him. Her teeth bit into her bottom lip once more.

Galen never looked away from her face as he took her hand in his, his fingers brushing lightly over her mound, and pulled their clasped hands to the side. "I love everything about you. How could you doubt yourself in this of all things?"

"I—" Her mouth gaped open, but no more words followed.

"Should we stop?" Galen leaned back, giving her space.

But just as quickly, Sylvie grabbed his arm and jerked him back against her. "No." She shook her head, some of the strength coming back into her features as she raised her chin. "If you left me again, I'd hunt you down to the end of lands."

His cock twitched against her abdomen, earning a soft gasp. *Fuck.* She could undo him so thoroughly without even touching him where he needed it the most.

"We can't have that." His forehead leaned against hers, the length of her braid tickling his bare chest, her nipples little pebbles against his skin.

Sylvie pulled their bound hands back to the apex of her thighs. "Touch me. Please."

It was all the invitation he needed. She released him to grasp his hip as Galen slipped his fingers into her sacred forest. Warm wetness greeted him immediately, and he groaned against her, burying his head in the crook of her neck. "You're so wet." He slid a finger between her folds, earning a delicate moan.

"You made me wait a long time." Her fingertips coasted across the muscles of his lower abdomen, making them clench in response. And then she found her courage again, her palm slipping lower to wrap around his length.

He bucked into her touch, loving the way she held him and the feel of her wrapped around his cock. "A mistake I don't intend to repeat," he all but growled against her skin.

"Then fuck me, Galen." She tugged at his length before releasing him. "Please."

He slid his fingers through her folds again, earning a little whimper as he grazed her clit. She was ready for him, and he'd never been more ready for anything in his life.

Galen wrapped an arm around her back, the other swooping behind her knees as he squatted to lift her.

"Wait!" Sylvie slipped away.

His heart nearly stalled in his chest.

"Don't hurt yourself worse. Lie down. Let me..." She licked her lips again and pushed her braid behind her, baring her chest once more. "Let me take care of you. Of us both."

Loathe though he was to admit it, she was right. Trying to carry her off as he planned would have been terribly painful at best, a mess of falling bodies and more injury at worst. Besides, he had no bed to place her on, no place at all really but the cold floor.

"As you command." He spied the blanket they'd shared the night before crumbled in a ball on the floor and stretched it out, laying it across the smoothest portion of the ground he could find. Then, Galen lay atop it, doing his best to keep weight and pressure off his injured limbs.

Whatever momentary shyness had gripped Sylvie when they'd undressed had vanished. She all but sauntered across the narrow space to him like the proud warrior he knew and loved.

Galen stroked himself as she approached, having no doubt he could come just from taking in the sight before him. He sucked in a breath as she straddled him, his whole body going tight and eager in anticipation.

"You're sure?" he asked, giving her one last chance to change her mind, to realize what a mistake it was to be with someone like him.

Sylvie batted his hand away and replaced it with her own, positioning him just at her entrance as she hovered above him. "I've never been so certain." Without another word, she slid down his length, moaning as they came together.

Stars danced in front of Galen's eyes. He bucked his hips, unable to stop himself as he gripped her waist and sealed them together. She was so tight, so perfect, like they were made for one another. Nothing else in all the world could be more right.

But then she moved on him, rolling her hips and sliding along his length, and he realized that the moment they came together was just the beginning, the first step into paradise. Nothing and no one had ever made him feel this way—not as a boy, clumsy and foolish, or as a man, still uncertain of what he wanted.

This was what he'd been yearning for all his life. His perfect match. His mate.

Sylvie planted her palms on his chest, her glowing eyes staring down at him as she rode him with all the fury and fight of the warrior she was, and Galen met her back just as fiercely, their bodies crashing together as he thrust up into her warmth. Her fingernails dug into his skin, not enough to break it, just enough to grant a sting of pain that somehow heightened his pleasure.

Her back arched, her breasts on proud display as she found a rhythm that fit them both, her delightful whimpers and cries a sign of just how much she enjoyed their coupling.

Galen's balls drew tight, his release near, but he refused to finish before her. He bit the inside of his cheek, willing himself to hold on and not spill inside her as he so desperately wished. She was close, her head thrown back, her eyes blazing. Her pert breasts teased him, begging him to suckle them and taste their pearled peaks, but that would have to wait. He wouldn't divert her course as she sought her pleasure with him, no matter how much he wanted it.

With a cry, she came apart, her body shivering and jerking under his palms where he held her tight to him. She soaked his length in her wetness, her core clenching around him until his sight blurred at the edges, and he finally gave in to his pleasure with a cry of his own, thrusting his hips up to meet hers in a frenzy as he spilled deep inside her.

Galen gasped for air in the last throws of his release. Sylvie all but collapsed across his chest, her breath on his cheek and a sheen of sweat across her skin.

Magic tingled through him, as strong and delightful as the after quakes of his release that still rippled through his form. A mating bond. He'd marked her, and her him. He didn't need to see it to know, to acknowledge what settled between them as Sylvie pushed up on her arms and stared at him with a look he'd never seen on her face before—pure pleasure and contentment.

"I marked you," he said, as if that wasn't obvious. But the horror of what he'd done, what they'd done, settled in his chest as he stared up at the beauty in his arms, his cock still lodged deep inside her.

She shook her head, her hair tickling his skin. "We marked each other."

"But you'll be—" *An outcast. A traitor. Exiled along side me.* He'd gotten so caught up in the moment he'd failed to consider the implications for her. He'd *failed* her. Again.

Sylvie placed a finger over his lips, silencing the words he couldn't bear to speak. "I chose this. I wanted this. I've never wanted anything so much." She raised off him and slid to sit on the blanket at his side.

Instantly, he missed being inside her, the longing to never be parted from her twisting tumultuously with his guilt.

"And it's beautiful, don't you think?" She gestured to the mark on each of their bodies, a blinding smile on her face.

The mark snagged his full attention, and Galen found he couldn't stop the smile spreading across his lips. It *was* beautiful—a small bird tangled in a nest of roses. So perfect and so apt. How the magic of their land always managed to choose so well, he couldn't say, but he could never deny that what they had together was its own beautiful design. If they only had this one time, this moment, it was worth it.

Sylvie pushed to her feet, and Galen groaned at the loss. As she walked a few feet away, he caught the sight of his seed on her thighs and had to bite back an entirely different sound that caught deep in his chest. *Fuck.* He never imagined the effect such a sight could have on him or how it could make his wasted cock spark back to the edge of life in an instant.

She cleaned herself off before picking up a little bag, the one from Leigh that he'd nearly forgotten about, and returned to his side.

"Now I can take care of you in a different way." She gave him a knowing look that only sparked his desire.

"You've given me too much already."

She pulled a little jar from the bag and raised her brows as she twisted the top open with a little pop. "That was too much?"

A deep chuckle slipped from him. "I think I can be your equal match in this too."

"Good. And here I worried I was going to have to challenge your stamina in a whole new way."

"I think I might enjoy that."

"Oh, I *know* you will." She winked.

Unwilling to break the ease between them or disrupt their new intimacy, Galen held his worries locked within as he watched Sylvie tend to his wounds.

"I should have done this first." Her cheeks flushed a deeper shade of pink as she took her time rubbing the ointment into his skin. The coupling had been fast and hard, but in this, she was gentler than a feather, her fingers barely teasing his skin as she tended to each wound—closed thanks to Leigh's magic, but still red, angry, and throbbing.

"The wait was worth it." *More than worth it.* He caressed her cheek, pushing back strands of her hair that forever fell free of her braid and would likely slip back over her pointed ears in moments. "I'd gladly take such a wound every day if it meant being with you like this. Besides, we'd waited long enough as it was."

Her task complete, Sylvie snuggled down beside him on the poor blanket of a bed, her naked body pressed against his side. "Far too long," she agreed. "But I don't want to see you in pain, especially not for this." She gestured between them. "I'd have you healthy." She pressed a kiss to his jaw. "Happy." Another graced the crook of his neck. "And by my side."

"I don't deserve you," Galen said, turning toward her and wrapping her strong, lithe body in his arms.

"Let me be the judge of that." Sylvie settled against him with a contented sigh.

For that brief moment, Galen let himself savor the woman in his arms and the bond they'd forged. He hated the risk and danger it would bring upon her and that he was the cause of it, but feeling her love and seeing their shared mark upon each other's bodies made his heart swell so fiercely it was liable to burst. Fates and kings be damned, he'd do whatever it took to keep her safe and by his side.

CHAPTER 13

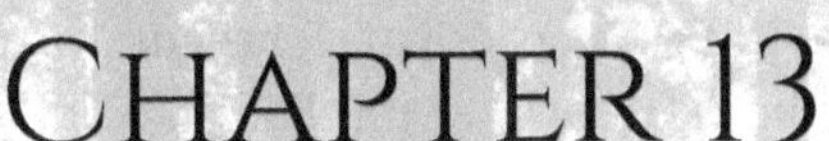

Galen drifted to sleep, content to linger in pleasant dreams with Sylvie still pressed against him and wrapped in his arms.

Until a shiver of magic rolled across his skin, jerking him awake. Sylvie roused at his side, likely having felt the same thing. Forest magic, by the feel of it, and familiar.

"Shit." Reality rushed in like a painful punch to the ribs. He should have known someone would come looking for them. They'd missed whatever happened between the kings. War? Death? They weren't terribly far from the site. He hadn't felt any great outpourings of magic to signal a massive battle, but with all his focus on Sylvie, he could have missed something.

Sylvie had already hastened to her discarded clothes and began tugging them on in earnest. Galen did the same. Whether a random patrol or someone searching for them, it'd be best to face them clothed and prepared.

"Let me handle them," Sylvie said.

Galen shot her a hard look. "They're probably here for me. I won't have you bear the burden of my crimes."

"But—"

"No. Please," he begged. "In this, let me care for you for once."

She swallowed thickly but nodded, still working on the last of her armor.

A loud whistling teased Galen's ears. Any doubt of who approached and why vanished from his thoughts.

He knew that tune well. It was one Ambrose, the king's Captain of the Guard, favored, especially when he was in an uncertain mood.

Of course he would come looking for them. To take Sylvie from him and order her to return to the Forest, to dole out a fateful decision upon him, or both, he couldn't say, but no outcome seemed favorable. For all that he cared for and respected the man, he followed the rules to the letter and was the king's trusted friend and advisor for a reason.

The whistling slowly grew louder, as if Ambrose took his time making his way to them and wanted them to be fully aware of his approach. When Galen could hear his intentionally loud steps through the dry underbrush, he stepped from the shelter with Sylvie not far behind.

"Ambrose." Galen crossed his arms.

"Galen." Ambrose nodded before coming to a stop a few feet away and staring past him. "Sylvie."

"What news of the battle?" Galen asked. If it still raged or had gone awry, Ambrose wouldn't be standing in front of them, certainly not look so hale and clean. He hadn't seen a fight, whatever had happened.

"Resolved without one. For now."

"And Wren?" Galen prodded. He needed to know her fate.

"Returned to the Court of Air with Sigurd."

A little of the tension sitting between Galen's shoulder blades loosened. He sighed. Wren was safe. Whatever she'd suffered at the hands of the Unseelie was over, done with. She could go home if she wanted or stay with the king she loved. Whatever her choice, he was glad she was free to make it.

"The Unseelie were freed as well," Ambrose added, his own arms crossing in front of his chest. "Riven was lenient, given the human was well, but I wonder if we won't regret that."

A bitter laugh caught low in his throat. Lenient with the Unseelie, but not with him? What a dark twist of fate.

But Wren was well, he reminded himself. Even if he suffered, her well-being was what mattered. She'd come into danger at his hand, and that she'd been delivered from it safely was a blessing he'd be forever grateful for.

"How did you find us?" Sylvie asked, moving to Galen's side.

Ambrose took a seat on a slanted rock, clearly not seeing either of them as a threat. "I felt you both leave the battle."

"You knew it was us?" Galen asked. It could have been any number of fae shifting from place to place.

"You think I wouldn't know the feeling of your magic by now?" He arched a brow. "Anyhow, I followed the direction you'd gone once things calmed down. Then, I felt..." He coughed, and that was all the indication Galen needed to know exactly what he referred to. He'd felt their bond settle into place. The captain's cheeks darkened beyond his thick beard.

Ambrose rubbed at the back of his neck. "Anyhow. Thought I'd give you both a little time to, err..." He waved his hand. "Then, I shifted to make sure you'd feel me and I wouldn't come on you both unawares. Seemed the respectful thing to do."

Much better than him stumbling in on them during the act. Not only had Ambrose been their commander as members of the elite guard, he'd become a father figure of sorts to Galen over the years. Being caught by Ambrose while mating with Sylvie would have been more embarrassing than if his own blood relatives stumbled upon them.

"To get to the point," Ambrose continued. "The king sent me. He wants to see you." His gaze slid from Galen to Sylvie. "Both of you."

Galen flung out an arm in front of Sylvie. "Don't punish her because of me!" He bared his teeth, all but snarling at his commander. "She would never betray the Court of the Forest. Sylvie only sought to help me." If he had to fight the man to protect her, so be it.

Ambrose stood quickly, raising his hands in front of him. "I'm just to deliver the message and bring you to Riven."

"It's okay." Sylvie grabbed Galen's arm, giving it a little squeeze. The smile she aimed his way hit like a punch to the gut. How could she be so calm? So fine with everything?

"But you—"

She squeezed tighter. "I made my own choices, and I regret none of them."

"Sylvie..." He dropped his arm before twining his fingers with hers. The time for regrets was passed. Now, they had to face whatever awaited. But whatever the king's judgment may be, Galen would do anything—promise anything—to ensure Sylvie didn't pay the price for his treasons.

"Fine." Galen pulled in a deep breath and turned his focus back to Ambrose. "Take us to the king."

CHAPTER 14

THE TERRIBLE KNOT STUCK in Galen's throat and refused to release as they waited outside the king's private office. Galen had been there more times than he could count—had long ago memorized the intricate design of great trees and wild animals carved into the double-door entry. Not once had he been so nervous. But then, his fate, and that of his mate, had never rested on what the king would decide once those doors opened and they were let inside.

They stood there in heavy silence, his fingers laced with Sylvie's, for no more than a minute or two, but those seconds could have been an eternity. Solona, the king's advisor, opened one side of the double doors and slipped out into the waiting area, her golden dress swishing across the floor. She paused briefly, her head tilting ever so slightly to the side as she looked at him before her gaze dropped to his and Sylvie's joined hands. Her expression gave away nothing before she gave a short nod and said, "He waits."

Solona gestured toward the office. Light spilled out from within, a beckoning harbinger, though whether of damnation or salvation, he couldn't say.

"Well, don't keep him waiting," Ambrose said with a pointed look Galen's way.

Galen's grip on Sylvie's hand tightened as he looked to her. She gave a weak smile in return, but he couldn't find the strength to return it, no matter how much he wanted to comfort her at that moment. Finally, he stepped toward the door, bringing Sylvie with him.

Ambrose moved into his path with a shake of his head. "Just you for now, Galen. Sylvie will wait with us."

Shit. Galen wiggled his fingers on instinct, trying to somehow tie him closer to the woman he loved. This was it. Already they separated them. He'd hoped to plead his case to the king before they were separated. But maybe, just maybe, a voice whispered in the back of his head, going in alone was a good thing. Perhaps they would spare Sylvie even if they planned differently for him.

Galen turned to Sylvie, who stood uncharacteristically silent and pensive. "It'll be all right," he said. For her, if not for him. If they planned to exile them both, they'd do it in one swoop rather than making her wait. Ambrose wasn't cruel. Neither was the king. Separating them now could only mean that their punishments were divided. If Sylvie was safe, he could face whatever came next for himself.

"Galen..." Her shoulders drooped.

"Hopefully, I'll see you in a few minutes." He tore his hand from hers before she could say something to make him crumble. His actions led to this moment. He'd face his fate head-on and with courage.

Without a backward glance, he entered the king's private office and slid the door shut behind him.

Riven waited in his chair behind the desk, hands folded under his chin and elbows propped on the desktop. A casual pose, but his expression was carefully blank, giving nothing away. Without being told, Galen crossed the room to stand a careful few feet away from the front of the desk and waited, his posture stiff, chin raised, and heart trying to beat right out of his ribs.

"Galen Lightstrider." Riven stood, his fingertips pressing into the desk top in front of him. "Former member of my elite guard, one who I specifically assigned to watch after my future queen."

The words hit like a dagger tossed across the space between them. The king hadn't just raised him up to the ranks of the elite. He was trusted. Assigned to bring Lia, the king's precious consort, to court and watch after her. Galen had prided himself on the honor, but hearing it tossed out now struck him completely differently, filling him with shame that nearly broke his resolve to meet his king's piercing gaze.

"A child of two courts," Riven continued, "but I always believed your heart and loyalty were here."

"They are, your highness." The words spilled out, met by a slight widening of Riven's eyes. "I was oath sworn to Sigurd in my youth, but I did not want it. I did not wish to serve him." Galen dropped to one knee and bowed his head. "In my heart, my loyalty was always with the Court of the Forest. With you."

Riven rounded the desk until Galen could make out the king's boots—clean and gleaming, free of any sign of the struggle that occurred earlier in the day—just a few steps away. Galen held absolutely still, the fine hair on the back of his neck prickling in anticipation of the king's next word or action.

"Lia believes this."

Galen's ribs squeezed tight in the heavy pause that followed.

"As does your mate, I'd wager."

At that, Galen's head snapped up to stare at his king. "She's innocent of any treason against the Court of the Forest. She did not know of my vow to Sigurd. Sylvie has done nothing to harm her honor other than give food and comfort to an exile." *To me.*

Riven rubbed a spot on his chest as he glanced away. "Love can make us quite impulsive." He glanced back at Galen. "I trust her loyalty. She will not be punished for her act of kindness."

A deep, gasping sigh whooshed from Galen's lungs, and he sagged toward the ground. "Thank you. Whatever fate befalls me, thank you for sparing her." She would be safe. Sylvie would be spared. Whatever punishment awaited him, he could endure it knowing that.

Riven leaned against the front edge of the desk and crossed his arms as he stared at Galen down the length of his nose. "You stole Sigurd's consort to atone for stealing mine and to prove your loyalty to my court."

"I did," Galen confessed.

"You didn't consider that might cause more problems for us?" Riven raised one fair brow.

"I should have, but I was desperate." So painfully desperate. And didn't that make fools of even the smartest among them? "I saw an opportunity to return to the Court of the Forest and to prove my loyalty."

"To whom?"

"To you." Galen swallowed. "And to Sylvie. She had to know that I didn't want to betray you or leave her. I love her," he said, surprised at how easily the confession flowed off his tongue now. "I had to see her again, even if just one last time. I had to make sure she knew."

Riven pushed off the desk. "I don't like the method of it, nor did Sigurd. Had the Unseelie not interfered, we might have a war on our hands." He paused, the silence painful. "But as it stands now, we have a tentative alliance."

Galen sucked in a breath. An alliance? It was more than could be hoped for between courts with so many years of animosity between them.

"Sometimes our worst mistakes can take a positive turn," the king continued. "Though Sigurd's mate, Wren, asked a favor of me before she left with the Court of Air."

Just the sound of her name had his shoulders hunching further. He'd risked her life, betrayed her trust. Whatever friendship he'd found was long gone.

"Do you wish to know what it was?" Riven asked.

"Yes, my king," Galen replied, barely a whisper. He needed to know as much as he dreaded the answer.

"Then rise."

On shaking legs that still ached from battle, Galen pushed to his feet, squared his shoulders, and met his king's steady gaze.

"She asked for mercy for you. For her friend who loved the Forest and did not mean to harm her."

Galen's mouth dropped open as the words echoed themselves over and over in his mind. *Mercy. Friend.* Tears stung the corners of his eyes, and he hastily blinked them away.

For the first time since he entered the room, a soft smile broke across the king's face, reminding Galen not of the monarch he'd served but the man he'd come to know and respect—Riven's true self beyond the guise of the imperious monarch he often donned for the court. "Anyone who can befriend the future queens of two Seelie Courts would be a valuable ally, especially one who is willing to risk exile to prove their loyalty and love."

The tiny spark of hope Galen had held tightly protected in his heart swelled in a rush, pushing out against his chest and filling him up from within. A tingling that had nothing to do with magic rushed under his skin as he stared at Riven with barely concealed wonder. "You mean..."

Riven nodded, his grin widening. "Welcome back to the Court of the Forest and my elite guard, Galen Lightstrider."

CHAPTER 15

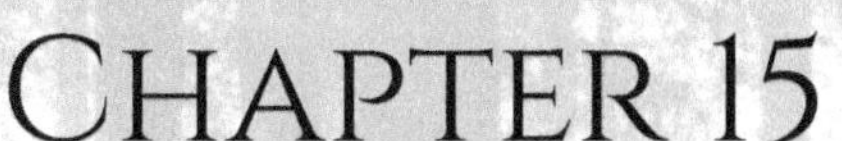

Sylvie

SYLVIE PACED OUTSIDE THE king's office, striding back and forth across the same wavy line on the rug that she stared at, all her thoughts with Galen beyond the closed doors. They wouldn't exile him again, right? Not after he tried to save Wren at great risk to himself. Or worse, they wouldn't— She shook her head, refusing to let her thoughts wander in such a dark direction. Sylvie nibbled on the edge of one nail before flinging her hand down to her side and chastising herself for the dozenth time about the bad habit. It didn't help that her nails were filthy.

Another glance at Ambrose and Solona, where they stood near the office doors, didn't help her mood. The two—frequently jovial and pleasant—kept their features carefully locked down, sharing furtive glances between one another, which held a multitude of things Sylvie couldn't discern. Neither would fully look at her nor answer her questions about what transpired beyond. Sylvie huffed in their direction and resumed her pacing. Some friends they were, keeping her in the dark on this of all things. They'd *never* done that before.

But then, she'd never aided and bedded a traitor before.

Sylvie sighed and slammed herself down in a chair.

He loved her. Damn it. If only it hadn't taken betrayal, exile, and nearly starting a war for him to confess and finally realize how much she loved him too.

But then, maybe if she'd just been a little bit braver, she could have told him before all of this mess and perhaps prevented some of it. Courage had never been an issue. She went after everything in life with gusto and often got it, too. Difficulty? Failure? Just more challenges to be overcome, and she loved a good challenge. There was little that got her quite so excited...except perhaps a certain male.

Sylvie rubbed her palm over the section of her clothing hiding her mark—not that her attire did anything to hide the magic of it, which she knew Ambrose, Solona, and Riven had certainly felt. Probably many others, too, once they'd shifted back to the capital.

Galen loved her. He had loved her for years as she'd loved him. Who fell first? Someday, hopefully, she'd get to ask him.

No, not hopefully. She would. In this life or the next, in exile or in the Forest, she would be with him. No act of kings or fate could keep them apart. She narrowed her eyes at the door Galen had disappeared through. Except maybe that. For now. Just for this moment.

If Galen were to be exiled once more, she'd follow. And if they tried to stop her? She barely choked down a maniacal laugh as it crawled up her throat. Let them try. It would be a challenge she'd relish.

Sylvie pulled her necklace from within her shirt, where it had rested against her chest, and held the little golden leaf in her fist. The magic of it gave a strong thump in the direction of the office, guiding her unerringly to the one she loved. Her mate.

She regretted little, only that she hadn't been more obvious in her desire. She'd dropped hints, plenty of them she thought, but then she understood Galen's hesitation too. It was the same thing that held her back for so long. Having him in her life, even as just a friend, was something she couldn't bear to be without. If she confessed and he didn't feel the same, it could ruin the precious thing they had. It took his exile for regret to truly take hold. She loved him, and he might have never known.

But now that he did, now that they were mated, nothing would prevent her from going after what she wanted. Never again.

The door creaked open, and Sylvie leaped to her feet. Breath caught in her throat as Galen emerged, eyes wide and glowing, King Riven just a few steps behind him.

Galen's gaze found hers and locked onto it. His chest rose and fell in heavy breaths. At the first slight upturn of his lips, she knew, like a spark bursting into flame.

She ran for him, heedless of those looking on, and leaped into his arms. Her legs wrapped around his hips, holding him close, never letting go, as his arms banded around her back, pulling her tight to him. Then her hands were on his face, drawing him closer still. The look in his eyes told her everything she needed to know.

He wouldn't die today. He wasn't exiled, and neither was she. They would have a life together in the Forest, the life she dreamed about.

Sylvie's lips crashed against Galen's, promising forever and savoring the blessing they'd been given. Mercy. Forgiveness. A new start. He met her back with enthusiasm, his joy and the glow of his magic consuming them in an aura of light. But it wasn't just his glow. It was hers too. Theirs. As beautiful and unique as the mark that bound them as mates.

Someone coughed, but Sylvie ignored them, kissing Galen with all the pent-up worry and emotion coursing through her. On a second, more robust cough, Galen finally pulled away, his eyes hooded and glassy, his cheeks flushed. Sylvie imagined she looked the same but couldn't give a damn if anyone knew or judged them for it.

Slowly, she slid to the ground, her legs a little wobbling and her whole body tingling with joy.

"I guess we should look for some new quarters for you both to share." Ambrose beamed with pride, not a hint of surprise on his face.

He knew, damn him. He'd known before he brought them there. Sylvie shook her head at him with a scowl, but he just shrugged.

"I trust you both will be content to remain here in the Court of the Forest?" Riven said, a broad smile stretching his regal features. Nearby, Solona shared a conspiratorial grin with him as well. They'd all known. *Ridiculous.*

"We would," Galen answered for them and then stared at Sylvie, the glow of his eyes still blazing. "If you're still content to have me now that I'm not an exile."

At that, Sylvie laughed. "As if you could get rid of me now. Of course, I'll have you. I love you."

Galen leaned in, his forehead pressed against hers. "I love you, too."

He loved her, she loved him, and the future had never been quite so bright.

The End

A GIFT FOR A FAE WARRIOR

MEGAN VAN DYKE

Author's Note: A Gift for a Fae Warrior

A Gift for the Fae Warrior is an optional prequel in the Courts of Faery series, and is set approximately six months prior to *A Bargain with the Fae King*.

Story Description

Aine's Day should be a time for celebration with family. But when the Unseelie dark fae launch a surprise attack, Galen will have to forego the festivities and fight to protect the Court of the Forest and the woman he loves.

CHAPTER 1

Áine's Day, the celebration of family in honor of the ancient Seelie queen, was a joyful time...for most fae. For Galen, though, it picked at old scars in a way that made his chest ache and urged him to hide from the world.

He shivered. The thick cloth of his guard uniform sheltered him from the winter chill but did nothing to warm the heavy emptiness in his chest. The grim thoughts were out of place, given the holiday. A whisper of festivity came from the outer yard. Fae chatted as they finished preparations for the upcoming celebration. But he couldn't bear to be in the middle of that all day.

Galen gave the horse one last, affirming scratch on his muzzle before pulling away. The mare snorted her disappointment, and he couldn't help the way his lips quirked up in one corner. She was such a needy girl. Truthfully, he didn't mind though. There was something calming about being with the horses. Trust and loyalty lay between them, something he'd strived for all his life with his fellow fae but never quite achieved.

Horses didn't judge the way fae did. They didn't see a fae of mixed heritage, only knew he tended and loved them far deeper than most.

He glanced toward the city of Virideria, capital of the Forest Fae, as he exited the stables in the outer yard. It rose like a mountain from the surrounding plains and forest, a towering mass of stonework and plant life more living than not. Tall trees stretched skyward, catching the last rays of the afternoon sun on their too-bare branches. Most of the year, the sight took his breath away. But with winter settled over the land, most trees had shed their leaves. The shrubs and vines lay dormant. No flowers bloomed.

It didn't help that the magic of the land was fading—painfully so. If it continued, the verdant land he loved would be gone, reduced to a near lifeless existence for all seasons and all time.

The occasional burst of high laughter carried far beyond the labyrinth-like city, a poignant reminder of the preparations underway. Even the nearby fae practicing in the yard were more jovial than serious, teasing and taunting one another.

In truth, he probably should have been in the city helping with preparations, but something about Áine's Day always made him sad. It was a celebration of family, of the great sacrifice of the last fae queen.

Before the numerous fae courts arose, there were only two: Seelie and Unseelie—the dark fae. Legend said the Seelie queen, Áine, so powerful her magic stretched her life far beyond what any currently living fae could comprehend, felt her days growing thin. It was time to decide an heir lest the magic choose for her upon her death. But she had many children and loved them all dearly. It was an impossible choice, as was leaving it for the magic to decide. There was already strife amongst her children, and she wouldn't pass into the aether only to leave behind war amongst those she loved.

So, the queen did the only thing left to do. She gathered the last of her strength and split the powers within her. She pushed out a piece of her magic to each of her children. In doing so, Áine faded away, but the various Seelie courts were born, her children their first queens and kings.

The holiday celebrated her sacrifice, her love for her family.

Bitterness teased Galen's tongue, and he huffed a sigh. He wouldn't be spending the holiday night with his family, as many fae did. He may have his parents' blood in his veins, but his true family was here in the capital amongst his fellow members of the royal guard. In fact, there was only one individual he truly wanted to spend the day with.

As if his thoughts conjured her, Galen caught sight of a figure stalking his way, blond hair shining in the sun.

Sylvie. Just the sight of her warmed him.

She waved, bouncing on her toes as she picked up her pace and jogged toward him. "There you are!"

Though Sylvie dressed as he and all the rest of the guard and was a head shorter than most, he never failed to find her, drawn by a pull that was as impossible to ignore as it was difficult to acknowledge. At least to her.

"What are you up to?" She planted her hands on her hips in what could be an intimidating stance if not for the broad smile that dimpled her cheeks.

His lips curled up in return, something they often did of their own accord in her presence. "Just checking on the horses."

Sylvie rolled her eyes. "As if you didn't already do that this morning."

He shrugged. Spending too much time with them was impossible, in his opinion anyway. Sure, there were plenty of grooms and stable hands, but as part of the king's guard, they were required to see to their own horses as well, build a bond between beast and fae. None of them seemed to enjoy that duty quite as much as Galen.

"You know me," he said.

"Yes." She winked. "I do."

And she did, better than anyone probably. Not that she could lie about it if she wanted to. No fae could. That was an entirely human ability, and humans were a rarity in the Court of the Forest these days.

"Anyhow." She dropped her arms and looked away, a touch of color rising to her cheeks. "I came to ask if you—"

A tingle of magic zipped across his skin.

Sylvie must have felt it too because whatever she planned to ask disappeared into the breeze as she turned toward its source.

A fae had appeared at the honing point, shifting there from somewhere beyond the capital. Somewhere far away, by the outpouring of magic that rolled across Galen's skin. A jump from somewhere nearby wouldn't generate such a powerful magical signature.

The newcomer collapsed to their knees, as if the shift had taken all of their magic and left them on the edge of consciousness.

The fine hairs on the back of Galen's neck rose.

Shit. No one would push themselves so hard unless there was trouble.

Not a word passed between them as he and Sylvie sprinted toward the honing point—magical shapes and symbols worked into the ground to aid fae in shifting from place to place. Those with the ability anyway. Only magically strong fae could shift at all.

The man on the ground reached for them, his other hand pressed against a smear of spreading crimson on his uniform. Galen recognized him now. Cirrio, one of the guards assigned to assist in the protection of Amantia and the human who resided there.

Sylvie gasped, drawing up short.

Something tight and terrible gripped Galen's chest as he dropped to one knee at the man's side. "What happened?"

"An attack! Unseelie in Amantia."

Close to the border. The Unseelie hadn't made it far, but their ability to slip past the protective wards and enter the territory of the Forest at all was troubling. More than.

Sweat dotted the man's skin. His breaths rose and fell in heavy gasps. It had taken all he had to travel so far—probably shifted in one movement. The nasty wound didn't help.

"We need a healer!" Sylvie yelled to the fae in the yard.

"Must tell Ambrose," Cirrio groaned.

"We'll handle it from here." Galen clasped the man's shoulder. The Captain of the Guard had to be informed at once, but Cirrio had done enough.

"Ambrose is meeting with Rivenean," Sylvie said.

The king. Good. Might as well tell them both at once.

She held out her hand. "Let's go."

Galen squeezed the man's shoulder. "Rest. You've done your job."

"There's more." Cirrio hissed in pain as the other fae neared. "They took Eugene."

A dark pit may well have opened up and swallowed Galen whole. Sylvie's shocked reply was no more than a buzzing hum as he digested the man's words. *The human.*

Of course.

There were so few left in the forest, all of them older, near the end of their years. It was the reason for their fading magic. By some cruel twist of fate, or ill magic of old, all the Seelie courts, even the Unseelie, had become dependent on humans to enliven their magic and thus the land itself. But many of the doors to the human realm within the Court of the Forest were closed. They had been for ages.

But as bad as things were for them, they were much worse for the Unseelie. Their last king died ages ago, taking the heart of their magic with him. Without a leader, and with few humans about, their magic grew stale, faded away to near nothing, and took the magic of the land with it. What remained was a hard, barren place with little life and less joy.

It was what would happen to the Court of the Forest if things didn't change.

Galen stepped back as other fae swarmed in to aid the injured guard. Sylvie grabbed his hand and laced her fingers through his.

Before he could savor her touch, she shifted them away.

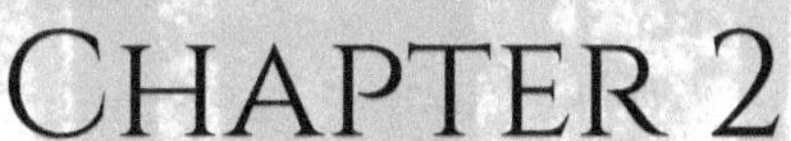# CHAPTER 2

T HE WORLD SHIFTED AROUND them in the blink of an eye. One moment they were in the outer yard; the next, they stood outside the doors of the king's private office. Such a short shift rarely took much time, and all too quickly, Sylvie dropped his hand.

But there was no time for remorse, not with news of an attack.

Rivenean Silvanus, King of the Forest Fae—or Riven, as he preferred to be called—no doubt felt them appear outside his office. He was king for a reason, succeeding his father at a young age to lead the fae of the forest. Ambrose, too, would have felt their approach. Still, Galen rapped hard on the wooden door to announce their presence. It was a courtesy, one of the rules he lived by.

A moment passed before Ambrose's deep, gruff voice rang beyond the carved doors, bidding them enter.

Galen pushed open the door and held it for Sylvie to follow.

The room was much as it always was—long and wide, with dark-barked tree trunks making up much of its walls. Tree branches arched overhead in a ceiling that wasn't completely enclosed. Only old magic kept the rains from touching the rich carpets laid over the stone floors or the ornate cushioned furniture that dotted the space, lending to comfortable conversations, even if the topic was less than relaxing. As one of the king's elite, royal guard, Galen often met in confidence with the king himself and his close advisors.

But today, the king wore an expression he didn't often don in private: wonder, excitement, and dare he say, hope? The fluttering of it caught in Galen's chest for a moment before the reason he was there smothered it.

"I do hope you're right," Ambrose said to Riven, finishing up whatever conversation they'd been having.

Riven leaned back in his chair. Rays of sunset spilled across his long brown hair where it tumbled over his shoulders, bringing out gold in the strands. He was the portrait of a proud, contented king in that moment, especially with the open archways behind him letting in a view of the sprawling city beyond.

The king poured out plenty of confidence for his people, his court, trying to be brave in the face of their fading magic. Only those close to Riven knew how dire their situation really was and how it ate away at the young king and his inability, thus far, to fix it. But not today. Whatever they discussed, it truly pleased the king.

Galen's throat tightened. And here they were, about to smother that joy.

"She has to be it." The king's gaze turned wistful. "I feel it."

She?

Sylvie cut Galen a quick look, the same question in her eyes, but there was no time to ask. Not now.

"What is it?" Ambrose asked, turning fully to them at last.

A bit of silver colored his beard, more prominent there than his dark brown hair, a shade similar to Galen's own. Ambrose had been Captain of the Guard many years before Riven became king, but that didn't mean age had taken its toll. Far from it. Ambrose still fought with all the physical and magical strength of youth. The captain could beat Galen in a duel, much as he was loath to admit it.

Galen cleared his throat as he shifted on his feet. "There's been an attack."

Riven's joy vanished in a heartbeat, replaced by an intensity that sent his eyes glowing green and his lips drawing back in a near snarl.

"Where?" the king and Ambrose asked at the same time.

"Amanita. It was the Unseelie." The word clanged in the air like dissonant bells vying for dominance.

Riven slammed his hand on the desk with a colorful curse. "Terrible timing."

Questions rolled unspoken across Galen's tongue. *Because of the holiday? Or because of whatever you discussed?*

"Aye," Ambrose echoed.

"There's more." Sylvie's voice rang with confidence. "The Unseelie took Eugene."

Riven and Ambrose went eerily still. Galen could have sworn the temperature dropped, and the nearby trees groaned in agony.

Ambrose broke the tense silence. "We go at once."

"Yes, sir," Galen and Sylvie answered in unison.

"I need to stay." Riven closed his eyes as a portion of the desk cracked under his palm.

Galen fought against the rise of his brows, aching to ask why. This wasn't like Riven. He'd expected the king to shift to the city the moment he heard their report, eager to cull the threat and see to his people. It was what he'd done before, other times the Unseelie had caused trouble.

Ambrose set his jaw but said nothing. That alone spoke volumes. He'd no trouble speaking frankly to his king. Whatever commanded Riven's attention—this *she*—had to be of the utmost importance.

Something heavy in his stomach turned over.

Change was in the air. Good or bad, he couldn't yet say.

"I have to see her again," Riven said to Ambrose as he opened his eyes, ones that glowed bright green with emotion. "If the Unseelie grow this bold, if the worst has happened to Eugene... We need her."

Sylvie's hand grazed Galen's, causing his heart to leap into his throat. He glanced at her from the corner of his eye, just in time to see her mouth, *A human?*

The question slammed into him like a key turning a lock. This *she*, this woman he knew nothing of before this moment, must have been a human. It was the one thing more important to the king than defending his territory—finding a young, gifted human who could help him revive it.

Galen's eyes widened in wonder as he gave a slight nod to Sylvie.

"Go now." Riven shifted his gaze to Galen and Sylvie, his voice carrying all the authority of his rank. "Capture the intruders if you can. Kill them if you must."

"At once, my king," they echoed again.

Galen grabbed Sylvie's hand, prepared to shift. The simple touch gave him more strength and surety than he'd ever admit. They'd go to the honing point first to conserve their magic in the longer shift to Amanita. They'd need all their strength for whatever awaited them.

"I'll gather more of the guard and meet you there," Ambrose said.

The last of his words still hung in the air as Galen and Sylvie shifted away.

CHAPTER 3

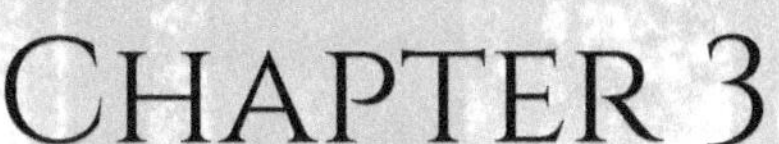

S CREAMING WAS THE FIRST thing Galen heard—a high, keening wail filled with such sorrow it pierced to his bones.

Fire licked up a building not far from the central square of Amanita, where they'd shifted to. Fae ran this way and that, several carrying buckets of water. Forest magic was little help against flame, a significant danger to the enormous trees looming around them. Many homes were carved out of the massive trunks or built onto their sides like mushrooms growing out of a log. Rope bridges connected the trees in a great web, the fire flickering precariously close to the underside of one.

Sylvie bolted toward a fae rushing in their direction. They wore the long robes that marked them a village elder, a fae of authority over the locale. She yelled something, her words lost as Galen tried to gain his bearings.

What Galen wouldn't have given for her ability to adapt so quickly, to rush into any situation with confidence. In battle, he could lose himself and let instinct take over. But in situations like this, he was always a bit awkward, taking too long to think through things and figure out the next step. He blamed that—and so much else—on his father. One too many childhood lessons on strategy, and his mind always rushed ahead before the rest of him, trying to plan steps in advance while leaving him standing still.

He gathered himself and raced after Sylvie. The flames were already dimming, snuffed by the efforts of the locals.

"More are coming," Sylvie assured the elder.

The older male wrung his hands in front of him, a vision of worry.

"Where are the Unseelie? Which way did they go?" Galen snapped. They had to find them. Stop them.

The elder startled. "That way." He gestured vaguely to the direction behind Galen. "Had to be more than a dozen of them."

Not many then, not really. A group that small couldn't conquer a village like this. They'd be vastly outnumbered, especially once word reached the capital. It must have been a targeted attack, a plan to steal the human.

The high, screaming wail he'd first heard when they arrived came again, cutting off the elder's words.

Galen turned toward a woman sitting in a heap on a grassy stretch of ground near the base of a tree. Long, dark hair tumbled around her shoulders as she hunched with her head in her hands and let out another sob. A second woman clung to her as if to provide comfort.

"She's hurt." Sylvie was off and running toward them in an instant. Galen started to follow.

But the elder said, "No."

Galen froze, twisting back toward the man.

"Eugene, the human," the elder clarified, though Galen already knew, "was her mate."

An ache built in his chest for the woman. It was a horrible thing to have someone you loved taken, and on a holiday to celebrate family, no less. His gaze glued to the woman drowning in her grief with Sylvie kneeling beside her. Eugene was old, his life near its end. The spark of magic his humanity provided to the Court of the Forest was dim already. It would be little help to the Unseelie hoping to revive their territory. Why take him?

"We'll do our best to get him back," Galen said. "Did they take anything else?"

At length, the elder tore his gaze from the woman. "Some food. A few tonics. Nothing important."

The typical Unseelie thefts. Taking a human though... That was new. Desperate.

He swallowed down the tightness in his throat. A nightmare.

Familiar magic rolled over his skin, leaving tingles in its wake. He didn't need to turn to know Ambrose and others had arrived from the capital.

"The village was busy with the last preparations for tonight's feast," the elder continued, his voice quavering. "They surprised us. Even the guards were caught unaware."

"Where are they? The guards?" Galen asked, dreading the answer. Only Cirrio had shifted to the capital. Whatever had happened to the others was a mystery.

"With the healers and seeing to the flames." The elder shifted on his feet. "We feared their return or another attack by the enemy," he said, as if trying to explain why they'd been called on, as if it was some failure of his leadership. Fool—that was the last thing to be worried about this night. Of course they needed to know and to help, especially since a human was involved.

Galen sensed Ambrose's approach before he saw him. Not his magic, exactly, though that was potent enough, but the man had an imposing presence all his own. Not that he was hard or cruel, far from it, though his appearance sometimes gave that impression, particularly the scar on the side of his face. Galen had never asked about the scar or its source, but whatever had happened, Ambrose was lucky it hadn't taken his life.

"Eugene was her mate," Sylvie said, returning to his side as Ambrose approached.

Galen nodded. To Ambrose, he said, "They fled that way."

"We'll go after 'em," the captain promised to the elder, echoing Galen's earlier words. A heartbeat later, Ambrose shouted orders to the members of the guard who'd accompanied him, his voice rising above the chaos.

Some he commanded to aid the villagers, most to go after the Unseelie.

"You two, with me," Ambrose ordered.

"I smell them this way," Argus, another member of the guard, said as they approached. His long hair was pulled back and bound behind his head like a horse's tail. A popular fae fashion, one Sylvie wore as well.

Not Galen though. He preferred his hair short and out of the way.

"I'll check the trees," Sylvie said before bounding toward one of the towering monoliths. She didn't need to be asked to use her magic, though it may have already borne some strain from traveling here. He felt it under his skin, a slight emptiness that only rest and time could replenish.

Galen couldn't help watch, entranced, as she placed her palm against the tree trunk and closed her eyes. A beam of fading evening light highlighted the planes of her face where it slipped through the dense branches overhead. It took effort to see through the eyes of the trees and view whatever images of the past clung to their bark. She wouldn't need to look back far, only a few minutes in time, but even that could be taxing.

It would be a lie to say he didn't envy the magic she was blessed with. A lie he could never utter, of course, even if he sometimes tried to tell it to himself—or he had when they were younger. He had his own abilities, but hers were rare, revered.

She'd been his bitter rival once. He'd never forget the first day he saw her. It was about two weeks after he enlisted in the guard. Or rather, after his father had all but forced him to. He'd resented the decision then, might still one day, but now...now the guard was his everything.

All the new recruits went through a series of trials and were ranked based on their performance. Only one member in his initiation group had bested him, a petite blond, thin and wiry, with little womanly figure to speak of. She'd stared at him as if he were an Unseelie, an enemy to be stamped out. He'd been no better, sizing up the woman he planned to best. Like it or not at the time, he was determined to be the best at whatever life forced on him. Her piercing look had cut through the space between them.

It slipped under his skin that day and had never left.

Somewhere along the way, it changed. Bitter competition turned to friendly rivalry, curt words to teasing banter. It was a slow slide. Years of change, so infinitesimal and subtle that he shocked himself one day after sparring with thoughts of what it'd be like to wrap her in his arms. Not to beat her in a duel but to press his body against hers and feel her writhe against him. Taste her lips. Discover how soft her pale skin was beneath her clothes.

Galen scrubbed a hand down his face, trying to pull those thoughts out with it. It was a wish he could never act on. Even if she desired him too—and sometimes he taunted himself with the hope that she might—he couldn't make good on it. Sylvie deserved better than him, a child of two courts who never truly belonged anywhere.

Still.

A moment later, she rushed back to them.

"They had him. About a dozen or so Unseelie, like they said." Her chest rose and fell in quick succession. "He was unconscious or asleep from what I could tell."

Galen's jaw stiffened. It was better than the human being dragged away kicking and screaming, especially given his age, but the whole situation grated against his senses. Capturing humans? He shook his head. He'd never have guessed they'd try something so desperate.

They followed the trail into the woods until Argus, the tracker with an exceptionally keen sense of smell, drew them to a halt.

"The scent splits," Argus said.

Galen's nose twitched as he sent out his magic, pulling at the air and tasting it. Argus was right. The presence of Unseelie wasn't a unique scent, not exactly, more of a wrongness that corrupted the area they'd ventured through. It wouldn't linger, but the presence of it in territory controlled by the Court of the Forest still raised the fine hairs on the back of his neck.

On instinct, he sought Sylvie. She'd already pressed her palm to a nearby tree, eyes closed and brows pinched in concentration.

When she cracked them open, Ambrose got straight to the point. "Well?"

She shook her head. "They did split up, but I can't tell which group took the human. It's too dark, the image too unclear."

Funny how trees couldn't see well at night. Or it would be if the situation weren't so dire.

"We split up," Ambrose ordered. "Track both packs. I believe you can take on a few reckless Unseelie."

A chorus of agreement rang out from the guard.

Pride swelled in Galen's chest. A few Unseelie on the run would be easy quarry.

Ambrose divided them up with a quick flick of his hand. "You all, take that way. We'll take this one."

Fae sped off into the trees, but Galen paused, a tingle of unease coiling through him. Sylvie gave him a weak smile where she stood a short distance away on the opposite side of Ambrose. Being apart from her on missions always made him worry.

"See you in a bit." She winked before hurrying after the others.

He swallowed the sudden knot in his throat. *Yes, just a bit.*

CHAPTER 4

T HEY MOVED WITH GRACEFUL speed through the forest. It was their homeland, after all. With a little help from the forest magic in his blood, he ran without tripping or stumbling over roots and shrubs in the dimming twilight. The land embraced him as one of its own, even if some of its citizens were less sure.

Ambrose drew them to a halt—one hand in the air and a flicker of magic across their skin.

Galen risked the use of a little magic to pull a subtle breeze to him. A myriad of scents floated through his senses, but there, among the pine and loam was what he sought, what Argus, still as a statue at Ambrose's side, had no doubt smelled as well.

Unseelie wrongness lingered heavily ahead like a thin fog of death.

And another scent so rare and sweet he scarcely knew it. The human?

Barely a sound rang through the night as members of the guard pulled free swords from their sheaths or bows from their back. The woman next to him nocked an arrow, creeping through the underbrush with silent precision.

The birds and bugs refused to sing in the presence of Unseelie. As if they, too, could sense the invaders in their midst.

Galen pulled the air as they drew closer. The scent was different this time—less foul Unseelie tang, yet the other presence remained.

"Something's wrong," he whispered, just loud enough for Ambrose to hear.

The captain looked to Argus, who dropped to a crouch, sniffing at the dirt.

"Ahead," Galen added.

Argus might not sense it yet. The younger fae could scent better than anyone, but only Galen amongst the elite guard could summon the air to his will, pulling the scent toward him rather than relying on what clung to the forest around them.

"The human lingers, but the others..." Galen gave a sharp shake of his head.

A dull glow seeped from Ambrose's eyes, the only hint of emotion he let show beyond his serious façade. "Move. Now."

They gave up all pretense of a quiet and careful approach.

Trees thinned. The risen moon cast its blue light across the group.

Ambrose was the first to spill out into the clearing that opened ahead of them. He went still for the briefest moment and uttered a curse before he vanished completely—shifted to something that lay ahead.

Galen caught sight of it a moment later. Ambrose appeared beside the prone form in the clearing. Without a thought, Galen sent out his magic, shifting to stand at the captain's side.

The old, human man lay still and silent in the grass, dead as the plant life around him.

Winter took the grass, as it always did. The man, however...

A gasp lodged in Galen's throat.

Ambrose knelt beside him, feeling for a pulse he wouldn't find. The man's hands were folded over his chest, a tuft of pine held in them. It should have been flowers. That was how the Unseelie sent off their dead, giving them back to root and soil. But in this late season, most flowers had all gone on.

The human's loss threatened to crush Galen into the ground, hollowing out his chest and gripping it tight at the same time. He didn't really know the male—not well. But humans were so rare, so precious and few.

And on this, an evening that should be full of festivity and family.

Leigh knelt opposite Ambrose, laying her hands on the man. She had the healing touch. Though Áine had long ago split her powers among the ancient founders of the modern Seelie courts, some abilities sprang up throughout them all, healing being one of them. Perhaps she realized even then the gift she granted to all fae, regardless of court.

Leigh wouldn't be able to save the man, not since Ambrose's grim look confirmed he'd gone on, but she might sense the source of his pain and passing. No obvious wounds marked him that Galen could see, nor did the air contain the tang of blood.

"His heart gave out." Leigh's shoulders drooped as her hand slipped from the man to rest in her lap.

Galen rubbed at his chin. "An accident?"

Ambrose shoved to his feet. "Must be. Even Unseelie wouldn't want to kill a human."

No, they certainly wouldn't. The man was no good to them dead. Though he'd have been little good to them anyway, old as he was.

"Do we go after them?" Galen panned his gaze across the surrounding trees. They must have realized the man had died and left him here with the best tribute they could give to his life in the circumstance.

"Aye." The word rolled from the captain like a tumbling boulder. "To steal a human and cause his death is unforgivable."

Indeed.

Ambrose turned to the others, ordering two to take the man's body back to the village.

"Can you scent where they've gone?" he asked Argus.

The younger fae already crouched among the tall weeds, nose twitching.

"They spread out, but"—he rose—"they went this direction." He gestured to the trees.

"Toward the border," Ambrose said.

Not just the border. Sylvie and the others had gone that way too. Galen stiffened.

The evening breeze ruffled his hair, carrying with it the distant aroma of the Unseelie. And if the wind carried their scent, it would catch his comrades' too—put them at risk of this pack of Unseelie catching their trail and sneaking up on them unawares.

He shared a look with Ambrose. The other man's eyes shone with the same concern.

Animalistic as they were, the Unseelie often had excellent natural senses like the animals they bore some resemblance of: horns, hooves, sensitive noses, and the ability to travel quickly over land. They must have selected some of their speediest members for this heist. That was the only explanation for why they seemed unable to catch up.

But everyone tired eventually, even Unseelie, and especially those in unfamiliar territory.

"Will you shift the winds?" Ambrose asked. "Throw them off course?"

Galen's throat tightened. It was one thing to use a little of his power here and there to scent the breeze. No one really noticed his magic when used so sparingly. But using foreign court magic amongst his Forest brethren always made him uneasy. He may as well have worn another court's colors for the attention it would garner.

Those around him knew about his heritage, of course, but reminding them was still unpleasant.

For Sylvie, though... Her face flashed before him.

For her, he'd do just about anything.

He nodded once, closed his eyes, and sucked in a deep breath. Powerful magic took all the concentration he could muster.

Galen reached within himself, pulling at the well of magic belonging to the Court of Air. Though he used it sparingly, the pool of magic was wide and deep within him, always begging to be unleashed. He sank down into its water now, let it roll under his skin before he gathered it to bend to his will.

With his eyes closed, he could almost see it as a tangible thing before him, a ball of magic and power tightly coiled and ready to be flung into the world. It writhed, willing and eager for his command. At length, he gave it, ordering the winds to shift, pushing them to the side, spreading his arms to cover an area he could only pray was large enough.

Magic poured out of him in a torrent.

It pulled at his body as he sent it forth, tugged and grabbed at him almost like physical hands, yearning for him to spend all he had.

Sylvie's face flashed through his mind, and he jerked the magic back, cutting off its flow before it could drain him dry. He couldn't become a liability. He wouldn't lie passed out in the woods while she was in danger.

The world around him returned as he opened his eyes. At some point, he'd dropped to one knee, though he couldn't say when.

A stiff breeze fluttered his hair—proof that the magic had worked.

Ambrose extended a hand and helped him to his feet. His arm remained on Galen's after he rose, their gazes locked. "Are you able to go with us?"

Even if he had to find a way to lie, he wouldn't be left behind, but the truth rose to his lips. "Yes."

"Good." Ambrose turned to the others. "Be on the ready. We don't stop until they're dead or out of our territory."

Galen took off with the others, sprinting through the trees. Fatigue grated against his senses like coarse bark, but he blocked it out, focusing instead on the captain ahead of him, a near blur where he moved through the dark forest.

The sound of battle reached them first—grunts, the clang of weapons. An animalistic roar shook the trees as figures took shape in the gloom.

He shifted forward, using his magic to propel him into the thick of the fighting. He appeared on the far side, just in front of an antlered Unseelie who fled the battle.

Galen pulled his sword and shifted his stance to meet his foe.

It wasn't pleasant, facing down a fleeing enemy with fear in their too-wide eyes. The tang of bile crept up the base of his throat. It wasn't right to kill someone on the run, but neither was the Unseelie raiding their villages, burning homes, stealing humans. His teeth ground together. No, for that and all the terrors they'd wrought over the years, the Unseelie deserved whatever came their way.

The Unseelie bolted, their long-legged, hooved stride carrying them away.

But even such powerful legs were no match for magic, a trait most Unseelie now lacked. Another member of the guard shifted into its path. With their focus still on Galen, the Unseelie never had the chance to see the new threat before the woman thrust her blade through her foe's chest and felled the antlered dark fae.

A guttural cry rang out and then went silent.

Less than a minute had passed since they'd arrived, and the battle was over. With the human already dead, the guard had no need for caution and plenty of desire for revenge.

Galen scanned the bodies on the ground—all Unseelie, though far fewer than expected. Perhaps the others had gotten away.

A small bit of the tension in his body uncoiled at that, even if they were his enemy.

With the immediate threat handled, he sought, as he always seemed to, the woman who occupied his thoughts more than he dared admit. As he looked from one form to another, the tension between his shoulder blades grew. His spine stiffened.

"Sylvie?" he called.

Ambrose drew up short, scanning the surrounding fae like a mother hen looking for her lost chicks. "Rainer is missing too. And Nithar."

A nearby guard wiped at the smear of blood—Unseelie by the wretched smell of it—on his face. "Two Unseelie ran off at the start." He pointed into the woods. "They went after 'em."

Three against two should be an easy victory. But...

He scanned the ground again. There weren't enough bodies, not nearly enough. This was only one group of the Unseelie, not both. And if the others were still out there...

Galen glanced back in the direction Sylvie had gone, his stomach bottoming out.

He slammed his sword into its sheath and sprinted between the trees.

Ambrose called after him. "Galen!"

Galen didn't stop. Couldn't wait.

If the remaining Unseelie stumbled upon Sylvie and the others, they'd be outnumbered. Even without the blessings of magic, Unseelie were strong—far greater in physical strength than Seelie fae—and Sylvie had already used so much magic seeing through the trees. She might not have enough left to flee or defend herself.

CHAPTER 5

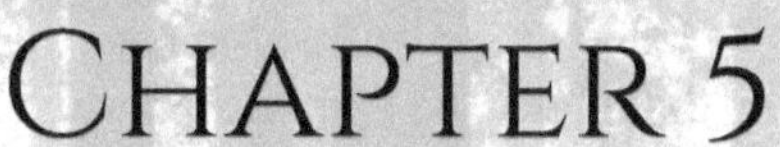

R OGUE BRANCHES CAUGHT AT his clothes and scratched his face. Galen raced without thought, without care, and without the typical grace of the Forest Fae.

Every second mattered. He had none to spare for stealth.

A familiar yell cut through the night like a knife to his heart. He stumbled and went down. Pain lanced through his knee, but it was nothing compared to the fear clawing at his throat. Galen got back to his feet and raced toward Sylvie in a heartbeat, ignoring every protest and ache of his body.

The clang of metal reached his ears, followed by a howl too eerie to be anything but Unseelie.

Moonlight filtered through the trees ahead, casting dappled blue light across shadows that sped, swooped, and slashed. He spotted Rainer first, facing off against two Unseelie but holding his own. Blood raced under Galen's skin as he sped through the trees, eying the other forms.

One dropped to their knees with a deep howl. An Unseelie with long horns yanked a sword free of the guard's chest.

Nithar. Shit.

Too late. Fury burned through him as Nithar fell to the side. The Unseelie turned away, focusing instead on another cluster edging toward a blond woman that fought with all the fury of a queen.

The dim light caught on Sylvie's blade as she swung it toward the approaching fae. Plant life rose up from the forest floor, heeding the call of her magic, but it did little to stop the approaching mass as they hacked through her constructs.

A large Unseelie crashed through the bramble and swung an ax against Sylvie's blade, sending it sailing. A deep bellow—Galen's own—cut through the night as he drew his sword and shifted in the same motion.

Less than a heartbeat later, he appeared between Sylvie and the enemy.

This time, Galen didn't hesitate. His foe still recovered from his swing. The Unseelie's eyes barely had the chance to widen before Galen swung his blade, connecting with the beast's neck.

Thick as it was, he couldn't cut through, but it was enough.

Blood sprayed. The body went limp and heavy, threatening to drag him down before he jerked the blade free.

Galen's chest rose and fell in one heavy breath as he stared down the advancing Unseelie.

"Who's next?" He barely recognized his own voice, the raw fury and threat coloring his words. He couldn't feel his body anymore or the exhaustion that had plagued him. The whole world narrowed to the enemy who'd tried to kill the woman he loved.

"Galen," Sylvie whispered. Surprise colored her words, not agony.

He didn't spare a look. She would be fine. Had to be.

But the Unseelie...

Galen shifted his grip. They'd feel pain before the night was over.

He rushed the enemy with a guttural war cry. Years of training took over. He moved purely by instinct, his body knowing what to do where only blinding rage filled his mind. Even his magic seemed to flow of its own accord, shoving out a powerful wind to knock some of the enemy back.

Again and again, he struck.

And then she was at his side. Her magic tingled across his skin before a skinny pine bent to her will, knocking an Unseelie away with a sickening crunch. Sylvie held a dagger in one hand as she slid around to guard his back, a stance they'd used so many times.

Galen rushed a thin, long-legged Unseelie.

Their blades crashed. Galen barely felt the impact. His opponent hissed at him, yelling some garbled threat Galen couldn't hear over the blood rushing in his ears. He swung again. The Unseelie dodged, leaping back with enviable speed, and snarled once more before sprinting off in the opposite direction.

Consumed by the rush of battle, Galen charged after her, blade at the ready.

A form shifted in front of him.

Galen sucked in a sharp breath, swung his blade, and stopped an inch from Ambrose's outstretched hand.

"Stop!" the captain yelled.

The command washed over him like an icy wind, taming his rage. A shudder wracked his body as he lowered the blade.

"Ain't losing any more of you running after those fiends," Ambrose said.

"But they..." Galen started. He couldn't think straight, couldn't form the right words.

Ambrose clasped him on the shoulder—hard. "I know."

The captain's gaze slid to the area behind Galen, and he finally turned, truly seeing the space for the first time.

Bodies and blood littered the ground.

Sylvie?

Galen's heart lurched then pulled back hard as he spied her among the other guards who'd arrived with Ambrose.

Safe. Alive.

He shivered in relief.

"Let them run home," Ambrose continued. "Let them tell how quickly we came upon them and the retribution we meted out."

Dimly, Galen recognized the wisdom in that, the gift of mercy their enemy did not deserve. But all he could think about as he crossed the space was Sylvie. "You're all right?"

Part of her hair had come undone and hung over her shoulder. Dirt and grime smeared her clothes. Even so, she gave him a tentative smile. "A few scrapes and bruises." She shrugged. "I'll live. Thanks to you."

Warmth crept up his neck, but he refused to look away. "I'm just glad I made it in time."

Sylvie bit at her bottom lip.

The action nearly had him stretching across the distance between them and pulling her into his arms. She'd hate that though, especially in front of the others. He could already picture her smacking him upside the face for coddling her.

"For a moment there..." She looked away, and a shudder wracked her form.

She didn't finish. She didn't need to. If he'd been a minute later, she might be dead, just like Nithar.

A knot tightened in his throat as he glanced at their fallen comrade. Another guard had already lifted Nithar's body, ready to bring him home. Fires would be lit in his honor, his ashes given to the ground to set free his spirit to return to the aether—a sorrowful end to what should have been a night of celebration.

Galen's gaze slid to Rainer, where he leaned on Leigh for support. Injured, but alive. He couldn't say the same for the Unseelie.

"We return to Amanita," Ambrose said, his commanding voice drawing everyone's attention.

"The Unseelie?" someone asked.

The captain rubbed at his beard. "We'll let the elder decide."

It was disrespectful to leave them where they lay, but so was stealing a human—it was a crime of the highest order. And they had their own pyres to light.

Sylvie slipped her hand into Galen's, and his heart skipped a beat.

He squeezed her hand in return, savoring the connection, the feel of her there.

She lived. If that was the only gift he received on Áine's Day, it was more than enough.

CHAPTER 6

WAILS OF MOURNING STILL rang in his ears when they shift-ed back to the honing point at Virideria. Their return to Amanita had been brief. Their allies had already returned with the body of the human, Eugene. The villagers worked to build a pyre to send his spirit on. After a few quick words of mourning and informing the elder of the fallen Unseelie—and the few who'd fled—they'd left the villagers to see their loved one on. It was a personal affair, and though a human was valuable to all, they hadn't known him, not like his family and friends had.

Exhaustion pulled at Galen. He shut his eyes against the lights of the city. The drain on his magic and ache in his muscles begged him to lie down right there on the ground. He seriously considered it, especially as Sylvie slipped her hand from his.

"You're back sooner than I thought," said an unexpected voice.

Galen snapped his eyes open. Solona, the king's advisor, stood just outside the honing point, smoothing out her skirts after having risen from one of the stone benches. She looked regal as always, the moonlight catching on the pale gown that stood out against her ebony skin and hair. She'd strung her halo of hair through with silver decorations that caught the light and glittered, likely in celebration of Áine's Day.

Her gaze swept over them, landing on Nithar's body. Her shoulders drooped.

Ambrose must have caught her look. "Aye. And there's worse than that. Riven?"

She shook her head. "The king is unavailable."

Galen's brows drew together before he remembered the brief bits of conversation they'd walked in on.

"With her?" Ambrose asked, crossing to Solona.

The hint of a grin twitched on her lips. When her reply came, it was quiet, almost too soft to make out. "Dream walking."

Sylvie's head snapped to Galen and tilted to the side. He shook his head in return—he didn't know the king could do that either. Though if the king was with this mysterious woman in dreams, not in the flesh, she must not be in their world. Not yet, anyway.

The hint of a headache built behind his eyes.

An Unseelie attack, a human killed, and the king possibly seeking another. It was all too much. The last bit offered the promise of hope—or crushing disappointment. Either could spell change. The burden Galen carried felt heavy as ever, and the drain on his body and magic weren't helping.

"You're dismissed," Ambrose boomed, turning back to them. "Bring Nithar to me," he added, thickness to his words. "We'll hold his passing rite tomorrow."

Galen retreated to the city with the others. A few revelers still trailed about, drinking and carrying on. He passed some in the halls. They were completely unaware of the attack the village suffered or the loss of its last human resident—that news could save until the holy day passed.

Near-scalding bathwater cleaned his skin but did little to remove the worries etched within him. He could only hope sleep would soothe that ache.

Better still would be a lover wrapped in his arms, but that was too much to hope for.

He retreated to his room within the royal guards' quarters. One perk of advancing to his station was the private sleeping arrangements, quite spacious and comfortable ones at that. Galen sank onto the side of his bed. Damp hair dripped down his neck, and he didn't bother to wipe it away.

Sleep called to him. He'd never been so ready to answer.

A knock on the door startled him from his stupor. It cracked open before he had the sense to speak.

Sylvie squeezed herself through the opening, her own hair still dripping and a clean, loose shirt billowing around her form. A smile softened her features, one that quirked higher as his gaze met hers.

"Hiding yourself away on Áine's Day?" she teased.

His lips quirked in answer. She could be a dream for all he knew. Maybe she was because the desire to sleep had vanished.

Even so, he answered, "I believe we missed the celebration."

"Well, maybe we can celebrate tomorrow." She pushed off the door and ventured near until she stood a few feet away. "I wanted to give you your gift today though."

"My gift?" he echoed, dumbstruck.

They'd never exchanged gifts. That was what family did, and though he thought of her that way, he'd have never guessed she felt the same. Sylvie actually liked her blood relatives.

"I'd planned to give it to you earlier today," Sylvie hurried on. She glanced away, a touch of color rising to her cheeks. "That's why I'd come to find you, but then the messenger arrived and everything, well..." She gestured between them.

He knew what she tried to say. Nothing about the day had gone the way they'd hoped or planned.

Sylvie pulled a small box from her pocket. Iridescent green paper covered it, shimmering in the light. A thin gold ribbon had been wrapped around the little box and tied in a bow that trailed off one side.

His throat grew tight. She'd even bothered to wrap it.

"I didn't get you anything," he stammered.

And, oh, how he hated himself for that right now. He'd considered it, more than briefly. Too many nights he'd lain in bed considering a potential gift before discarding it in his mind. What could you give to the perfect woman? What would she accept? What wouldn't make things awkward between them?

In the end, he never could decide, and now it was too late.

Sylvie giggled, her eyes bright with mirth. After all she'd seen and suffered that day, and no doubt as exhausted as him, she still managed to laugh.

He stared at her, too stunned to move, and then she did the moving for him, leaning in and stretching on the tips of her toes to plant a kiss on his cheek.

Galen's entire body went rigid.

Time seemed to slow as her soft lips pressed against his skin in a gentle caress.

He'd give anything to freeze that moment, to bottle it up and store it away to relive it time and time again. Her scent lingered as she pulled back, leaving him lightheaded and swaying on his feet.

"You saved me today." Her words pierced the haze of the spell her kiss had woven over him. "That's a tremendous gift, and I won't forget it anytime soon."

The sincere adoration in her eyes was almost enough to bring him to his knees.

"You'd have done the same for me," he said, voice thick with emotion he'd yet to fully process.

Her blush deepened as she glanced away and pushed wet hair over one shoulder.

"I would have." Sharp little teeth tugged at her bottom lip. "Anyhow, here's your gift." She shoved the box in his direction, nearly smacking him in the chest with it.

Galen took it, holding it like the precious object it was.

"Well, aren't you going to open it?" she asked, finally looking back at him.

It'd be a shame to ruin the pretty wrapping but even more so to miss whatever was inside. The last gift he'd gotten—a bottle of elderberry wine—was from his parents. He hated the stuff.

One stiff tug at the golden ribbon sent it spiraling to the floor. The green paper, folded with perfectly sharp corners and an even precision that spoke to Sylvie's perfectionism, gave way with a quick rip and followed the ribbon. The box itself was simple and wooden—unremarkable.

However, when he opened the box, breath caught in his throat. A poplar leaf wrought of gold lay on a small cushion.

"It's an earring," Sylvie said. She may as well have pulled the question straight from his mind.

"I bought the pair of them." She pulled a necklace he'd never noticed before from the inside of her shirt. A twin of the leaf within the box hung from the cord around her neck. "They didn't... Well, I..."

Her lips pinched in the face she made where she wanted to lie and couldn't find the words to work around it. It was a trait he relished in her. So many fae could dance around a lie with ease, circumventing the magic that stuck the words to their tongues, but Sylvie often faltered.

"Anyhow," she hurried on, "you might hate it. You don't have to wear it."

"I'll wear it with pride." The emotion already swelled in his chest and tugged up the corners of his lips.

Galen pulled the earring from its resting place and fit the clasp through the hole in his ear. It'd been years since he'd worn one, not since his early days in the guard when he'd worn a token of his father's. Did Sylvie remember that? Time, and Galen's strengthened loyalty to his king and fellow guards, had shredded the lingering ties between him and his father, but the earring hole remained.

Now, it'd be vacant no longer, and it was only fitting that a gift from Sylvie replace the old one he'd long since disposed of.

"Well, I should..." Her words trailed off as he dropped his hand, revealing her present glimmering at his ear. She blinked rapidly before sucking in a deep breath. "Well, I should tell you it's enchanted."

She rubbed her own leaf between her fingers and looked away again.

Galen's lips quirked up in the corner, and he fought against the rise of his brows. *Enchanted?* She could bewitch him mind and body and probably wouldn't care.

"In what way?" he asked.

"They're a bonded pair. One can always find the other." Her fingers slid over her leaf. "Touch it. Do you feel it?"

Hesitantly, he pressed the earring between his fingers. A faint warmth pulled at him, the gentlest tug toward the woman across from him.

Though truly, that feeling was nothing new.

She'd held her own gravity where he was concerned from that day at the trials long ago.

"Yes, I feel it," he said.

"Good." She dropped the necklace and tossed her hair once more. "If I'd given it to you earlier today, I might have been able to find you instead of getting into trouble. Or you could have found me faster."

His lips parted.

Her eyes widened. "Not that you didn't find me fast enough. You... I'm so grateful. Anyhow, it should help us if the Unseelie are going to continue to be a threat," she rambled on, but he could see the truth her words so cleverly tried to hide.

Yes, it would be helpful for them in doing their jobs as members of the royal guard. But more than that, she wanted to be able to find him and him to find her. If anyone in this world was going to track him down, he wanted it to be her. "I'll always find you," he promised and touched the earring once more.

Sylvie drew silent, staring at him, the emotions flickering in her gaze unreadable. Her throat bobbed.

The air between them grew thick and heavy.

That gravity that had nothing to do with the enchanted earrings pulled Galen toward the petite woman across from him. He should profess his feelings.

Tell her all the thoughts racing through his head and the way her gift made him feel.

Take her in his arms. Kiss her.

"Well..." Sylvie faked a yawn—her real ones were never that restrained. "It's late. I need to rest."

His heart lurched. He stepped toward her, but she'd already spun on her heel.

"See you tomorrow." She waved and flashed a grin over one shoulder before hustling out of the room entirely too fast.

Galen was left staring at the empty doorway she hadn't bothered to close behind her.

He waited. She didn't return.

A sigh slipped from his lips as he collapsed back onto the edge of his bed.

As always, he made his decision too late. A wry grin lifted the corner of his lips as he rubbed the earring between his fingers again, feeling the slight pull in the direction of Sylvie's room. Maybe tomorrow he'd finally gather the courage to tell her how he felt.

Maybe.

But one thing he was sure of: he'd remember this Áine's Day for the rest of his life.

MEGAN VAN DYKE

DESTINED
FOR THE
FAE KING

Sneak Preview: Destined for the Fae King

Curious about what's ahead in book 3, Destined for the Fae King? Check out this preview featuring Lysandir, prince of the fae Court of Fire.

Sneak Preview: Destined for the Fae King

To most in the Court of Fire, it was a day like any other, but to Lysandir, it was one of the last precious normal days before his future would be irrevocably upturned. Worst of all, he knew it and had been able to do nothing to alter its course.

Warm air drifted through the open terrace, ruffling Lysandir's hair and stirring the envelopes splayed out on the table before him. The temperate weather of the Court of Fire usually comforted him, the spice-tinted breezes off the Sand Sea especially, but not today as he picked up each letter in turn, reading over the family names carefully scrawled in ink upon each one's front.

Lysandir held a crimson envelope in the air, letting it catch the light coming in through the windows behind him and watching the paper shimmer like a smoldering ember.

He expected to feel something as he read them over and over—sometimes silently and others aloud—some pull, some indication of which woman would shape the court's fate.

His visions often gave him a little glimpse into what was to come, but they were fickle in their comings and goings. Very rarely, he could beg and plead with the fates to show him something he wanted to see. Though the last time he'd done so, what he saw affected him so thoroughly that he vowed never to do it again. Other times, however, visions slipped in like the breeze, teasing his thoughts and offering images of the future when he wasn't expecting them. Often the visions were benign or so obscure he couldn't make sense of them.

One; however, had been anything but.

He knew what it showed the moment he glimpsed it, and now time and fate were drawing it closer to realization. No matter how he wanted to change things, or at least prepare for them, he had not found a way to stop what was to come. Lysandir flipped through the invitations again, hoping that this time something might tell him which woman was the one from his vision. Her family's name had to be there, but none of them stuck out in any helpful way.

"Have your visions deduced my future bride?"

Lysandir all but dropped the invitations as his head jerked up at the sound of his brother's voice. Lost in thought as he was, he hadn't felt him approach. Sheer curtains still fluttered in the wake of Vasilius's entrance as he strode across the room, resplendent in his gold and red attire, a few shades brighter than the dark auburn of his hair. Lysandir's brother was king of the Court of Fire, and it was time that he fulfilled the age-old tradition of their court by selecting a consort from one of the gifted families loyal to the Court of Fire. The names of each family line was inked on the invitations he held, waiting to be sent via the human emissary to the respective families. Each great house would send their most suitable unwed daughter to try for the king's hand.

If Vasilius had his way, he would have ignored the tradition completely. But Lysandir's mother, Vasilius's stepmother, wanted it done. It was her wish, possibly her last given her advanced age, and though his brother was short-tempered, impulsive, and all the things a king could be both praised and damned for, at least he gave the dowager queen the respect she deserved and honored her wishes in this. After all, it was quite the thing for a human woman to reign as queen consort for so long, birth a fae royal, care for another as her own, and outlive her mate to achieve years marked in the nineties. Young for a fae—unusually old for a human.

"You will choose your bride," Lysandir reminded his brother. "Well, you, mother, and the council." At least they had the wisdom not to leave the choice entirely up to the king.

Vasilius plopped down in a chair across the table, throwing one leg over the armrest, always the picture of refined yet casual arrogance. "Ah yes, my *human* bride."

The disdain in his words left a sour note on Lysandir's tongue. His brother's aversion to humans always sat poorly with him, especially where this matter was concerned. If it had been Vasilius's sole decision, he would have chosen a fae mate, at least for now. He had plenty of lovers to pick from, none of who wanted to share his brother with a human, even if it would greatly benefit the court and his reign. Only their mother's insistence that she'd see him mated to a human before her death swayed him. And thank goodness Vasilius respected her as much as if she'd birthed him, even though he was older than her in years. Whenever his brother's scorn of humans rankled him, Lysandir made it a point to think of his mother—a human—and the way Vasilius loved and respected her. If it could happen once, it could happen again.

Though that, too, twisted him up in knots when tied with his visions. Lysandir shook his head, trying to clear the thoughts that never failed to trip him up. "We need humans," he reminded Vasilius. "You know that. As king, it's your responsibility to—"

"I know. I know." Vasilius cut him off with a wave of his hand. "But they're so..." His features twisted up in a frown. "What if they only send the hideous ones?" He gave a dramatic shiver.

"Doubtful," Lysandir leveled him with a flat stare. It was an honor for the families to send a human woman to vie for the king's hand, and no respectable gifted family would miss the chance to have a future queen come from their lineage. They would send their best, however much he dreaded it. *She* would be among them, the woman he'd seen whose family name had to be on one of the invitations.

"Then why look so dour?" His brother taunted. "You like humans more than I do. Perhaps they'll be one you can pluck up for yourself... After I've had my choice, of course."

If only he knew.

But Lysandir had not shared his vision with anyone, least of all Vasilius. Sharing what he saw only seemed to make it more certain, and this... He had to find some way to change things, though time was quickly running out.

"I suppose we'll see," Lysandir slid the envelopes together, tapping their sides until they made a neat stack.

His brother rolled his eyes and shoved himself out of the chair. "It would do you well to take a lover or four." He planted his hands on the desk and leaned in, eyes gleaming. "There's nothing quite like the hunt and savoring the thrill of conquest."

In your opinion. Lysandir thought, but held his tongue and kept his features as neutral as possible. Arguing against his brother's promiscuity would only urge him on. Instead, he gave the letters one more tap and set the pile aside.

Vasilius sighed, shaking his head. "I planned to invite you on a little hunt with me today, actually." Vasilius tugged at his gloves as if they didn't fit, though everything they owned was tailored to perfection. "Don't worry." Vasilius gave him a sideways smile. "We aren't searching for cunt."

Lysandir stiffened, sitting a little straighter in his seat. When his brother wasn't searching for his next bedmate, he was generally plotting something much more reckless. "Don't tell me you're going to the border."

Scattered Unseelie had been spotted there recently, though none had yet to test their wards or cause much trouble as they had with the courts of Forest and Air. Lysandir clenched his jaw, waiting for and dreading a response.

"Of course," Vasilius replied. "I think it's best to send a strong message now rather than wait for them to try something against us, don't you think?" The gleam in his eyes said exactly what kind of message his brother wanted to send—the kind that turned Lysandir's stomach.

The recent Unseelie activity was a threat, to be sure, but he'd returned from the Court of Air not long ago and hoped for some respite from danger and trouble before his brother dragged him into some mess. Vasilius didn't even seem to care that he'd nearly become the prey of a nasty beasty and literally poisoned himself to try and prevent what he saw coming. His brother hadn't even asked why he'd entered the competition, as if he'd gone for sport and nothing else. Not that Lysandir would have told him if he asked. This vision was a burden he'd bear alone, at least for now, not while there still might be a way to avert its course.

Lysandir sighed and rose from his chair with a shake of his head. He gave one last lingering look to the pile of invitations. Maybe he should chuck them in a fire, but no, someone would simply remake them. He could *lose* one before they were sent, but which? Or would that only make the future he dreaded more certain?

"Well, are you coming or not?" Vasilius asked.

"Fine," Lysandir ground out before pulling himself away from the invitations. If only to keep his brother from worse trouble. The moment the damned letters were out of sight, some of the tightness in his shoulders released, the burden of the future set aside for a little longer.

He might as well make the best of this time before the women arrived. They might be the only bright days he had left.

ALSO BY MEGAN VAN DYKE

The Castamar Duology

The Musician and the Monster (Beauty and the Beast)
The Artist and the Dragon (Sleeping Beauty)

Reimagined Fairy Tales Collection

Second Star to the Left (Peter Pan)
The Ugly Stepsister (Cinderella & Snow White)
The Alice Curse (Alice in Wonderland)

The Courts of Faery

A Gift for a Fae Warrior (Optional Prequel)
A Bargain with the Fae King (Book 1)
Bound to the Fae King (Book 2)
Forgiving a Fae Warrior (Book 2.5 - Optional Novella)
Destined for the Fae King (Book 3)
Marked by the Fae King (Book 4)

Stolen Empire

Captive of the Stolen Empire (Book 1)

ABOUT THE AUTHOR

Megan Van Dyke is a fantasy romance author with a love for all things that include magic and romance, especially fairy tales and anything with a happily ever after. Many of her stories include themes of family (whether born into or found) and a sense of home and belonging, which are important aspects of her life as well. When not writing, Megan loves to cook, play video games, explore the great outdoors, and spend time with her family. A southerner by birth and at heart, Megan currently lives with her family in Florida.

Connect with Megan

www.authormeganvandyke.com
www.authormeganvandyke.com/newsletter/
facebook.com/AuthorMeganVanDyke
instagram.com/authormeganvandyke
tiktok.com/@authormeganvandyke
bookbub.com/authors/megan-van-dyke

9 781955 532471